Robin of the Wood
LEGEND

Adam Greenwood

Author's Note

It is said that no creative effort, whatever the medium, is ever finished, just abandoned. I have found this to be true, not least when it comes to writing a book.

Long after I finished the original version of this book, published as "Robin of the Wood", I continued to think of extra details of the world in which it was set and back-story for the characters, some of which I wrote down and tried to work into other stories.

Now that I have a chance to expand upon my original work, I have decided to include some of this extra detail and information. I hope it enhances your enjoyment of the story but most of all I hope you enjoy reading it as much as I enjoyed writing it.

Lythe and listin, gentilmen,
That be of frebore blode;
I shall you tel of a gode yeman,
His name was Robyn Hode.

A Gest of Robin Hood
c. 1492

I can noughte perfitly fit my pater-noster, as the
priest singeth, but I can rymes of Robin Hood and
Randolf Earl of Chester, as neither of owre lorde
nor of owre lady, the leste that ever was made.

The Vision of Piers Ploughman
c. 1360

So many are the tales told of Robin Hood,
perhaps all are true or perhaps none. Or perhaps, instead, the truth lies
in that strange land between fact and myth.
In the place where history becomes enveloped in the mist of legend
so that one cannot be told from the other.
The hero with a thousand faces. A myriad of tales told over many
centuries. So many stories, over so many years, surely cannot all be
about one man? Or can they?
He is Robin; the hooded man, Robin Goodfellowe, Robin of the wood.
As much a part of the forest as the leaves on the trees or the ferns which
grow at their foot.
His story takes place in a time outside of our own, what some call "The
Dream Time", others "long, long ago" and others, simply, "Once upon
a time".
Trapped forever within his tranquil purgatory, he awaits the time when
he can make restitution for his sin.
A protector of the weak, defender of the defenceless.
The hope of the world, yet the hidden from it.
Read these tales and take heed, for much of what is true is contained
within fable.

The Storm

The wind howled through the bare branches. Branches which had been stripped of their autumnal foliage by the gales and the rain which lashed down, soaking the ground and flooding out the burrows of the small animals which now cowered together, sheltering in hollow logs, under roots and any other covering they could find to protect themselves from the elements.

To one seeing such a storm for the first time, it may have seemed as if the end had come. It was certainly the worst storm for a generation, possibly even a century. Many ancient trees would be lost before the night had passed, many homes and dwellings destroyed but the forest would survive. The scars would heal and new trees would grow. New people would come to the forest and make their homes there. The animals would return, find new dwellings for themselves and dig new burrows. For, you see, such a tempest as this is not an end but a transition.

One man understood this. He had seen many before, far worse, and expected to see many again before the end.

Proud and tall, he stood in the torrential rain, the winds causing his hair and cloak to billow around him. Undeterred by the immense elemental forces, far greater than any mere human could possible withstand, the man stood with his arms outstretched as if to embrace the very storm which was tearing apart his surroundings.

The wind was a wind of change, blowing away the sins and mistakes of the past. The rain was washing away the old order of things. Everything was soon to change. The old era would pass away that night and, as the sun rose in the morning, a new one would begin.

"A bad business, this." muttered Clem, gazing sorrowfully at the dregs of ale at the bottom of his mug. "Terrible business. The miller's daughter vanished like that. Robbed and murdered likely as not."

"Let up with your gloom!" Seth retorted. "Comely lass like that? With that golden hair of hers? She'll 'ave run off run off with some rich lad from the town."

"Aye", Clem shook his head despondently, "I still say it's a bad business. Very bad indeed."

Despite how accustomed he had become to his friend's tendency towards morbid ramblings, there were evenings such as this one when Seth found Clem very difficult and rather tedious company so he welcomed the distraction when the inn door creaked open and the stranger walked in.

It was not uncommon to see folk from the neighbouring towns and villages in this tavern, situated as it was on the main trade road. A good share of its business came from letting rooms to weary travellers, glad of a good meal and warm bed before continuing on their way. The locals welcomed the opportunity to speak to them, share stories and hear any news they brought.

Standing in the doorway, the man looked around for a moment or two before approaching the bar.

"A pint of your finest ale!" he smiled at the barman with a smile which did not extend to his eyes.

Taking a small suede pouch from under his travelling cloak, he loosened the drawstring which sealed it at the neck and shook a few coins onto his palm. He handed the coins to the landlord before secreting the pouch back from where he had taken it.

"Have you a room for the night, my good man?" he asked, pleasantly enough. The barman's smile flickered momentarily but returned as soon as it had gone and, if he noticed at all, the man thought nothing of it.

"'Fraid not squire", replied the burly but kind-faced landlord, "but there's another inn not four miles down the road, and it's early yet. You should try there."

"But it's already dark outside," protested the man, "and the path leads directly through the forest. I daren't travel alone in the forest after dark!"

He realised that the barman seemed to be starring at him intently, making him feel rather uncomfortable. He met his gaze as the landlord spoke again.

"An honest man has nothing to fear in the forest."

The man suddenly realised that all eyes in the bar were upon him.

"But," he protested, "the place is crawling with outlaws and bandits!"

"An honest man has no need to fear them," Clem informed him, "They never lay a finger on anyone under the protection of the hooded man."

"The hooded man?" asked the stranger.

"Aye", said Seth, relishing the opportunity to join the conversation. Above the bar, carved in wood, was a relief depicting a heroic figure, proud and handsome with a longbow in his hand. Seth pointed out this carving to the traveller. "The Hooded Man, the good spirit of the forest – Robin of the wood!"

At the mention of a good spirit, the traveller's face had broken into a broad grin, so amused was he by this peasant superstition.

"You'll forgive me", he said, letting out a hearty chuckle, "but I'd sooner turn back than place my life in the hands of this fairy tale!"

"Robin is no fairy tale!" retorted Seth, warming to his subject and more than a little irked by what he saw as this stranger's derisive impertinence. "Every day of my life since the age of eight I have walked through that forest to the market and every day, at morning and evening, Robin has walked beside me. Never once have I been robbed or even threatened."

"Have any of you actually seen this man, this spirit beside you, with your own two eyes?"

"No, never with my eyes," Seth admitted, "Although some have." The traveller now sat listening with rapt attention, his incredulity of a moment before all but forgotten. "But I see him with my heart," continued Seth, "I know that he is there by my side, watching over me."

"So you know he is there despite not seeing him?" asked the stranger, a slight note of incredulity creeping back into his voice. "May I ask how?"

"When you know, you just know", Seth replied patiently, "but that's not the most important thing. What matters most is that the others know he's there too."

"Others?" the traveller asked, "What others? If you walk in a group then surely you're less likely to be robbed. Those villains look for easy pickings!"

"It's the villains I'm talking about!" snapped Seth, "All the people of the forest respect Robin and will not harm one who's under his protection!" He paused for a moment to down what remained of his ale before adding, without looking at the stranger, "I and all the men here owe our lives to him a thousand times over."

The other men at the surrounding tables had gradually abandoned their private conversations to listen to Seth recount the legend of the Hooded Man. At this statement, they heartily chimed in their agreement. The stranger drank the last of his ale and gently placed the mug down on the bar, a thoughtful expression on his face.

"Well", he mused, not directing his words at anyone particular, "I do need somewhere to stay for the night and it is still quite early." He looked up at the landlord. "Can you promise me," he asked, watching the landlord intently, "on your word and in the sight of God, that what I'm being told is true, not a joke at the expense of an outsider? This is not just my property at risk, it could well be my very life in the balance."

"I promise you, before almighty God," the landlord replied, looking the traveller in the eyes with an expression every bit as serious as his own, "that an honest man has nothing to fear in the forest."

The man looked at the barman for a few moments longer, studying his face for any hint of a lie, but he saw none. He reflected for a short time longer before decisively making up his mind.

"I'll go", he announced, "and trust this Robin of yours to guide me safely to the inn beyond the forest."

Taking his leave of the landlord and patrons, he bade them farewell and left the inn to continue his journey.

Outside the tavern, he untethered his horse, gave her a comforting pat on the neck and climbed up onto his cart. They set off at a gentle trot towards the forest.

The half moon which had shone brightly, clearly illuminating the path ahead, disappeared above the dense green foliage of the grand and imposing oak trees.

The traveller could see nothing. It seemed that not a single ray of light was able to penetrate through the leaves. He shivered despite the warmth of the air and pulled his travelling cloak tighter around his shoulders.

An owl hooted in the tree, totally at home in the darkness. There was a rustle in the undergrowth, a small animal of some kind making a dash for its burrow. As he made his way slowly through the forest, the traveller could feel a thousand eyes watching him from the blackness.

As the traveller struggled to make out shapes in the darkness his senses became more acute to compensate for this temporary blindness. Gradually, he became aware of an extra set of footsteps beside his horse, soft at first but becoming more and more distinct the further he travelled.

Slowly, very slowly, a very faint soft green light began to glow, showing the outline of the mysterious figure who walked beside the horse, leading it along the safe path. The traveller couldn't make out any features but there could be no doubt that this was Robin, the good spirit of the forest the villagers had told him about.

The fear and anxiety that had built up in his heart in the darkness quickly ebbed away as the traveller began to relax, trusting Robin to take him safely to the other side of the forest. The green light became brighter and more intense, lighting the path in front of the horse and enabling the traveller to see his mysterious companion.

The figure wore a dark green cloak with a hood which obscured his face. The cloak stopped a hand's breadth short of the path but the traveller could see no feet. A gloved hand swathed in brown leather held the horse's bridle and a flash of rough, unbleached sleeve could be seen where the arm disappeared under the cloak.

The horse quickened her pace as the light became brighter and brighter. The traveller gripped the side of his seat tightly, the fear beginning to rise in him once more. The horse galloped faster and faster, still led by the cloaked figure who now seemed to be almost flying beside her. The normally gentle and nervous beast was galloping at full speed through the thick forest, swerving round trees and avoiding the ditches as if she knew the path by heart, completely trusting the mysterious figure who guided her deeper and deeper into the forest. Suddenly they came to a complete stop.

The horse fell silent and the traveller released his grip, struggling to catch his breath. The figure let go of the horse and turned to look at the traveller who instantly understood the origin of the green light which now surrounded them bright as day.

The figure had no face beneath his hood, just a pair of bright green eyes which glowed with an intense heat, illuminating the forest where they stood. Eyes which burned into the traveller's very soul and saw all that was in his heart.

The next morning, an abandoned cart was found outside the inn beyond the forest. When the villagers started to move the sacks on the back they found the body of a young woman. A beautiful girl with long golden hair, murdered for the few coins she carried in her little suede pouch.

Yes. A bad business this. After all, an honest man has nothing to fear in the forest.

Willow looked towards the sun, it was already hanging dangerously low in the sky. She had promised that she would be home before dark and her mother would be worrying about her. This was the first time she had been allowed to go to the market on her own and she didn't want it to be the last!

She'd had a wonderful time exploring the various stalls and seeing the amazing range of intriguing goods available there. She had bought herself a small figure carved from a single lump of wood. It was not beautiful or even particularly well made but something about it had captivated her and she just had to have it. It was a figure of a man in a green tunic and cloak. When she looked closely she saw that his eyes were painted a deep, dark green just like her own.

Hastily, she pulled out from her basket the list that her mother had given her of things she was expected to bring back. A loaf of bread, a ham and some flour for baking bread and the cakes her brothers so enjoyed. She hurried round the relevant stalls and made her purchases then headed towards home on the path through the forest, her hair in its thick black plaits swinging gently behind her as she walked.

Mother had warned her that she should never walk through the forest after dark but the other path was so much longer and, after all, she had a fair amount of time yet before the sun completely disappeared.

As she walked beneath the mighty oak trees, Willow remembered her little wooden figure and took it out of her basket to have a closer look. The face was very crudely carved yet had a very definite expression, strong and noble yet strangely melancholy as if he carried a great pain that Willow could never understand. She stroked his painted hair and wished she knew why he seemed so sad. Although he was nothing more than a simple wooden toy she felt as if he was in some way alive, as if he knew she was there. Carefully, she tucked him into the pocket on the front of her dress.

Looking around her, Willow realised that she had been so absorbed in her little wooden man that she had wandered from her normal path and didn't know where she was. She swung around, desperately seeking a familiar tree or landmark but she found none. Dusk was falling rapidly. She knew it would soon be dark and then she would have no chance of finding her way out before morning. She would be forced to spend the night at the mercy of the forest. She ran this way and that, looking for the path she had lost but she could not find any trace of it. She sat down at the foot of a wide, majestic oak tree and began to cry.

A sudden noise startled her. A large man, who must have been sitting in the branches of the tree, dropped down and stood in front of her. He was joined by another man who emerged from behind another tree.

"Now what have we here?" Asked the first man, an unpleasant smile forming under his rough beard.

"Seems we have a little wood nymph who's lost her tree!" laughed the other man who was younger, and uglier than the first. "I wonder why she's so sad?"

Willow scrabbled to her feet, alarmed by these strangers. She pushed back into the tree, wondering how she could get away. The men came nearer and were joined by another, a short man with a patch over one eye. All three men were dressed in clothing that had once been grand but had become shabby from years of crude repair and were smeared with mud, dried blood and many other unidentifiable stains. Willow knew that these must be some of the outlaws she'd heard stories about. Men who lived in the forest, surviving by poaching deer and robbing unwary travellers who were foolish enough to wander into their domain.

"Perhaps", said the first man, "it's that basket she's carrying. Perhaps it's too heavy for the poor little thing?"

"Well we can't have that!" The short man exclaimed. "Let's relieve her of the burden!" He started towards her, his arms outstretched to grab the basket out of her hands.

"She might have an heavy purse too," laughed the ugly young man, "Let's see if we can't lighten her load!"

The old man pulled out a knife from under his jerkin. "Would be such a shame to leave a little waif like this wandering lost in this big dark forest." He turned to Willow with an evil leer. "Don't worry, little girl", he snarled, "You won't have anything to worry about very soon!"

Screaming, Willow dodged out of the way as he lunged at her with the knife. She tried to run but the tall man stuck out his foot and tripped her up. She fell, cutting her knee on a tree root. She knew there was no hope of escape. She was going to die.

She looked up, terrified, as the man with the knife loomed over her. He raised the knife and she closed her eyes, bracing herself for the blow but it never came. The other men gasped and Willow opened her eyes to see her attacker pinned to a tree with an arrow which seemed to glow with a faint green light.

Another arrow, its head burning with a bright green flame whizzed through the air and through the heart of the tall, bearded man. The ugly man began to run and was felled by an arrow through his back.

Getting up shakily, Willow looked around for the mysterious archer who had saved her. Even as she did so she saw that the arrows were starting to fade, as if melting from existence, leaving no visible wound. The body of the outlaw who had been pinned to the tree slumped to the floor and she saw her rescuer.

A few feet away stood a man who seemed to glow with the same green light as his arrows. He was tall, dressed in a dark green tunic and cloak, which blended with the forest around him, and held a longbow in his hand. Willow stared at him. Although she had never seen him before he was somehow terribly familiar. She looked at his face, framed by long brown hair which wafted gently in the breeze that blew softly through the trees. She looked at his eyes which, like hers, were a deep, dark green. She saw in those captivating eyes a sadness which she knew she had seen before, then suddenly she realised – this was her wooden man. The figure she had bought from the market was an effigy of this mysterious greenwood guardian.

She rushed to him, her fear and the pain in her knee forgotten, and held up her arms to be lifted. The bow melted as the arrows had done and he took her up with one strong arm. He said nothing but smiled at her as he picked up her basket with his free hand. She knew that she was safe with this man, if indeed he was a man, and that nothing could harm her now.

He put his finger to his lips to indicate that she should never tell anyone what had happened that evening, then he gently stood her back down on the leafy ground. He knelt so that their faces were level and placed his strong arms gently around her shoulders.

The faint light that radiated from the mysterious man grew stronger and at the same time, the forest around them began to fade. The light grew ever brighter and the forest less distinct and Willow felt as if she were wrapped in a warm, green cloud. She had a strange sensation of being no place at no time, as if she existed outside the normal bounds of reality. The light became dazzling, all she could see. A light that bright should have been painful but it was not. Instead, it filled her with joy and made her feel like she would never feel sadness again.

She closed her eyes and felt herself falling, slowly and gently, as if sinking in a warm pool, until she felt a softness beneath her she first took to be the leafy forest floor. She stretched out her fingers and they brushed not the crinkly autumn leaves she had been expecting but the warm fuzziness of a hand-woven blanket.

She opened her eyes to see that the light, the forest and her woodland guardian were gone. She was lying peacefully on her bed in her family's cottage, her basket from the market by her side. She could hear her younger brother playing in the tree outside. She sat up to see her mother standing at the stove, preparing ingredients for baking.

"Hello", she said, "I didn't see you come in! Did you get the flour?"

Willow took the basket over to the stove then returned to her bed. She remembered her little carved figure, the figure of the man who had saved her from the murderous outlaws. She felt in her pocket and, to her alarm, felt that it was not there. She prayed that she had not dropped it in the forest in her panic. Tears began to well up in her deep green eyes. She looked around frantically and saw the little man standing, proud and sad, on the small table beside her pillow, a silver ring set with a gleaming green stone laying invitingly beside him. Gasping with delight, she slid the ring onto her forefinger, delighting in the way it twinkled in the lamp-light. She picked up her little man and stroked his hair again. She gave the little wooden figure a gentle kiss and placed him under her pillow.

She knew that she would never forget her forest saviour. She also knew deep in her heart that he would never forget her. Even if she never saw him again, she knew that he would always be watching over her, guarding and protecting her. She knew now for certain that she would always be safe in the forest.

Marian

It was one of those strange, ethereal autumn mornings. The kind of morning where you can feel the tingle of magic in the air that makes you question whether you have actually woken up of if you are still dreaming.

It was market day in the town and Marian was heading out from the hamlet with her brother Rufus, a basket slung over her elbow. The pair were singing happily as they walked along. Although he was a good three years younger than Marian, Rufus liked to feel that he was his sister's protector and had insisted that he accompany her to the market.

The path that they were on, like all the paths leading out from the hamlet, led through the forest. The early morning autumn sunlight was shining through the treetops, speckling the path with polka dots of light and bathing the whole forest in a warm green glow.

Her singing ceasing abruptly, Marian stopped and put her finger to her lips, telling Rufus to be quiet.

"What is it?" asked Rufus, surprised at his sister's sudden change of demeanour.

"Just listen!" Marian replied, placing a hand on his shoulder absent-mindedly.

The forest was alive with sounds. The wind rustling the branches of the trees, branches which were inhabited with twittering and singing birds. Squirrels leapt from tree to tree and rabbits scurried through the undergrowth. As far as Rufus could tell, there were noises all around. He could not imagine which noise amongst the cacophony his sister wanted him to pay particular attention to.

Looking at him, Marian furrowed her brow.

"Don't you hear it?"

"Hear what?"

"Just listen," Marian told him. "Listen carefully. Try to hear through all the normal sounds. Do you here it?"

Listening very intently, Rufus tried to block out every sound, the rustling, birdsong, even his own breathing; all the noise that he was used to hearing. He tried to listen for something else, something that didn't belong amongst the woodland hustle and bustle.

Frustrated, he almost gave up. Then suddenly, he heard it.

A soft tune was floating on the air, a haunting, ethereal sound. A simple folk tune but played in such a way that the pair found they didn't so much hear it with their ears, but rather inside their heads.

The music had a hypnotic quality to it.

"Wait here!" Marian instructed Rufus, her hand pressing distractedly on his chest. Rufus was indignant!

"No way!" he cried, "Do you think I'm going to let you go wandering off on your own? Goodness knows what's out there!"

Although she tried to be understanding and often appreciated his assistance and presence, Marian couldn't help being amused by her brother's defensive behaviour. She knew that he saw himself as her guardian but there was something about this music which called to her. She knew she had to find its source and she had to do it alone.

"I'll tell you what," she soothed, "You go onto the market, get what we need and I'll be here waiting for you when you get back."

Still appearing unsure, Rufus opened his mouth to protest some more but Marian fixed him with the look she had used since he was a toddler, which always meant she insisted on having her own way in whichever argument they happened to be engaged. Rufus knew better than to argue with "the face".

Leaving her brother to deal with the practical task of acquiring food for the family, Marian ventured from the path and into the depths of the forest, following the sound of the music.

The music led her deeper and deeper until she found its source.

Beneath a tree, a man sat, playing a strange wooden flute. The ethereal music seemed to surround him like an aura. So absorbed was he in the music that he did not see Marian watching him.

The air was still, yet the man's hair seemed to flutter as if in a breeze, perhaps blown by the wafting notes themselves. Marian could not quite put her finger on why, but there was something unnatural about him. As if he was both less and at the same time more than a normal man.

He seemed real enough, sat with his back against the gnarled bark, his clothes were finer than those of a peasant but not so grand as to make him a lord. Dressed in earthy greens and browns, with his long brown hair and forked beard, he almost looked as if he could be a part of the forest itself, yet somehow he appeared out of place, as if he did not belong to this world. Marian struggled to see what it was about this man's appearance that should give her such an impression but she could not.

The tune came to a gentle close and the man lowered his flute to his lap. He looked down for a moment or two, as if contemplating the instrument, before looking up, not at anything in particular but just gazing into the distance as if renewing his acquaintance with his surroundings.

Suddenly, Marian realised that he had seen her. His face immediately expressed alarm but this quickly melted into a beautiful warm smile of welcome. He stood up and held out his hand to Marian, beckoning her to come closer.

Tentatively, she stepped forward. Despite this man's unearthly quality, she did not sense any danger from him. In fact, his presence made her feel safe and protected.

"You play beautifully"

"Thank you," the man replied, giving a little bow but never taking his eyes off her. "I've had a lot of practice! Are you alone?"

Normally, such a question coming from a stranger in the forest would have alarmed Marian, but not now.

"My brother's gone ahead to the market. I just had to find out where that beautiful music was coming from! My name's Marian."

The man's green eyes twinkled as he took her hand in his, kissing it lightly.

"A delight to make your acquaintance," he smiled, "They call me Robin."

"Do you live in the forest?" asked Marian, inquisitive to know more about this mysterious greenwood man.

"You could say that," he replied, a cryptic smile playing around the corner of his mouth, "If living is the right word. Surely you've heard the tales of Robin Hood?"

"Of course I have!" Marian replied, "Everybody has."

Marian narrowed her eyes.

"Are you trying to tell me that you are Robin Hood? Protector of the forest?"

Robin gave another bow, his arms spread wide with a flourish.

"The very same!"

"But Robin Hood's just a folk tale! A myth! Stories told by superstitious old folk to credulous children! I'm afraid I stopped believing in such things a very long time ago."

"Who'd have thought that one could become so wise in seventeen years!"

Marian got the distinct impression that she was being teased, then the fact suddenly hit her that she had never mentioned her age. How could this man possibly know? A lucky guess? She opened her mouth to challenge him but he spoke before she had the chance.

"I know many things Marian. Things you could never know and things you have forgotten."

His face took on a serious tone.

"Do not presume that a child's understanding of the world is inferior to yours simply because it took less time to form. Sometimes, the most important truths are best grasped simply, without complication. The more you know, the less easy it becomes to see the truth. Do not suppose that because something is a fantastical tale, it cannot also be true."

To Marian's great relief, Robin smiled again. She was so worried that she had offended him by her incredulity.

"Of course, not everything they say about me is to be believed! If I took all the stories of my heroic exploits to heart, my head should probably swell so as to wedge between these two trees!" He patted the hefty trunk of a towering oak by his side, "But that's the thing about legends. They tend to take on a life of their own!"

Pausing for a moment, Robin looked up at the sky before returning his steady gaze to Marian's beautiful face.

"You're brother will be waiting for you. Go to him. But come back and see me again!"

"How will I find you? The forest is so vast!"

"Your heart will show you the way." Robin replied. "Take this. Any forest dweller who sees it will know that you are under my protection."

He held out his hand, which Marian was sure has been empty moments before, and opened his fist to reveal a silver ring set with a translucent green stone which shimmered with an ethereal beauty.

Marian tentatively took the ring and slid it onto her finger.

"It's beautiful!" She exclaimed.

"As are you," replied Robin, kissing her hand once more, although this time his lips lingered a little longer. "Now go. You shall see me again before too long."

With that, Robin vanished. He did not walk away, he simply melted like a wisp of cloud.

As she stood staring at the spot where he had stood, the silver ring on her finger, Marian's heart beat fast in her chest. Partly it was the excitement of meeting this enigmatic, legendary figure, the hero of her childhood. Partly it was the shock of seeing him vanish before her eyes, but mostly it was due to the new feeling she felt.

She had never felt this emotion before but she did not need to be told what it was. She knew exactly what the stirrings in her soul meant.

She was in love.

As the months turned to seasons and the seasons turned to years, the love between Robin and Marian grew. Although at first only able to snatch precious moments together away from other mortal eyes, each could feel their soul entwine with the other, until existence apart seemed an utter impossibility.

As time passed, Marian became bolder, sometimes spending whole days away from home with her immortal beloved, exploring the forest, learning its mysterious secrets and meeting the strange beings that inhabited Robin's world.

Then the day came.

Feeling as if her throat were being shredded by iron barbs, Marian awoke in the night, coughing harshly. Looking down at her bed, she saw that the thin blanket she slept under was flecked with splatters of blood. She knew what this meant. The same had happened to her mother and within a year she was dead, her grandmother apparently likewise.

Her coughing awoke Rufus. In an instant, he was at her side.

Trying to appear brave for his sister, Rufus held her tightly as she sobbed into his shoulder, occasionally coughing dark red specks onto his unbleached nightshirt. Neither of them spoke. There was no need.

Gradually, Marian's attack subsided and she fell into a light, but mercifully restful sleep.

Although his sister did not realise that he knew, Rufus had heard the tales circulating amongst the minstrels and story tellers that Robin Hood was now most often to be seen in the company of a beautiful, golden haired lady – a lady they had christened the Queen of the Greenwood. These tales, coupled with his sister's frequent long absences, had been all he needed to make the connections and understand the truth.

Over two years had passed since the fateful day when they had heard the ethereal music in the forest, when his sister had run off to find its source, only to return with a mysterious smile and the unmistakeable glint in her eye of a young woman in love.

Following their father's death when Rufus was barely past his thirteenth summer, he had become the man of the household and when their mother had passed away also, barely a year later, he had assumed total responsibility for his sister's welfare and he took his role seriously. He knew that if anyone could help Marian, it would be her mysterious greenwood lover. He must take her to him.

The next morning, Marian seemed better. Although slightly pale, her beautiful face maintained its smile and her eyes had a glint of vitality. But as evening came, the coughing returned. Worse this time than before. Rufus wrapped her in the stained blanket and, gently picked her up. To a man of sixteen, used to carrying logs felled from the surrounding forest to the market, carrying Marian in his arms, even over some distance, presented little challenge.

Somehow he knew, when he lay her on that fallen log in the depths of the forest, that he would not see her again, not this side of whatever lay beyond the mortal world. She had fallen asleep as he walked. He stroked her hair gently and gave her a final kiss on her cheek which was flushed and hot from the coughing. He returned to the cottage with a heavy heart.

In time, Marian awakened to find Robin by her side, holding her hand.

"My life is nearly over, my lover." she whispered softly.

"Don't talk like that!" said Robin, although he knew in his heart that she spoke the truth. The radiant glow of life, which had always surrounded her, was already starting to fade.

"It's true, Robin. I've seen this too many times before. I don't have very much longer left to live. But you have shown me, in the last two years we've been together, more than I could have hoped to see in a thousand mortal lifetimes."

"If there was anything I could do..." Robin began, but Marian interrupted him gently.

"It's my time," she told him, "You've shown me that all life has an allotted season, and now mine is drawing to a close. But," she gripped his hand tighter, "There's nowhere I would rather be and no one I would want to share my last days with more than you."

Bending down, Robert took her face in his hands and kissed her. He may not be able to feel the warm sensation of a loving caress, but she could. His kiss was a gift of love. An offering with nothing expected or hoped for in return.

"Perhaps," he faltered. "Perhaps there is a way our love can live on beyond you, as a child."

"But," Marian looked intently at him, "You're a spirit, you have no mortal body. Besides, I will not live so long as to bring a child into the world."

"Love," replied Robin, "is more powerful than any obstacle, physical or mystical. Watch."

He knelt down on the soft earth. A single fern, which was dead, dry and blackened, lay, almost forgotten, in the scrub. Robin laid his hands over it and the plant was surrounded by a warm green glow.

Sitting up, Marian leant forward to see what Robin was doing. As he pulled his hands away, she saw that a new green shoot was growing from within the remains of the old.

"There needs only to be a tiny spark of life left," explained Robin, "for a new life to grow. That plant," he indicated the new fern, which was already beginning to unfurl its leaves, "is simply a recreation of the original and in its time it will wither and die. Such is the way with simple life."

He took Marian's hand.

"Our child would be so much more. The greater part of both of us, created with pure love. And they would not age and weaken as other mortals do. They would remain forever, an eternal testament to our love."

Marian looked away, a sadness coming over her face.

"Does that mean they would be like you?" She looked at Robin imploringly. "Unable to feel? Unable to share the simple physical pleasures us mortals take for granted? I love you Robin, but I would not wish that on any child."

Robin took her face in his hands and stroked her cheek tenderly.

"They would be our child, Marian, with not only the finest spiritual qualities of both of us, but the physical too. A mortal body rendered immortal."

"But I have only a few weeks, a month at most, left to live! A child, even an immortal one, surely cannot be born of a dead mother!"

"Look at the fern", Robin pointed. Marian saw that it was already fully opened. Young and fresh, certainly, but it had achieved many days of maturation in the space of a few short minutes.

"The life force of the child will keep you strong and feeling healthy until your last breath. This is the greatest gift I can offer you. Your last days spent happy with me in the forest, awaiting the birth of our child with joyous expectation."

Taking his hands and leaning forward, Marian kissed him passionately. His lips were warm although she knew he felt only the force of the pressure from hers. No taste, no tingle of nerve endings registering a lover's touch.

"I wish I could stay here with you forever," she told him, "though if I cannot, it will be a beautiful thing to die knowing that the child of our love will live on forever."

Words can only go a little way towards describing what happened next, and if anyone had been watching, there is no knowing what they would have seen. It was as if Robin became a part of Marion, fusing with her very soul. She could feel him inside her being, looking out through her eyes, touching the rough bark of the fallen log with her hands, savouring the texture, and the feeling of the warm breeze against her cheeks.

Gently, Marian's hands were placed on her belly, over her womb. She felt infused with the same green warmth which had vitalised the fern only minutes before. She felt a stirring in her being, and a quickening in her womb. The green energy receded until it remained only within the new child, the baby she would carry for the rest of her mortal life. She felt strong, energised, and all trace of the illness which would continue, unseen, to sap her mortal life, was gone.

She stood up, bursting with life and vitality. Robin was by her side. She took his hand and they walked together deep into the forest to enjoy the days which were made even more precious by the knowledge they would be cut short.

The thought of Marian's impending loss was like an icy blade through Robin's heart but, for her sake, he put it as far as he could from his mind. One day, she would be gone but today she was here, they were together, and they were in love.

A Child is Born

Knowing she had a minute at most left to live but determined to see her child, Marion strained to open her eyes. Even as she felt the life force ebbing from her body, she sat up, her back braced against the mighty oak tree, and held out her arms.

Gently, Robin placed the newborn baby into her hands and she pulled the child towards her chest. Blinking her eyes to clear the tears, Marian looked down at the baby nestled contentedly in her arms. Her little girl.

Although she had known that her child would not be entirely human, for how could she be when her father was an immortal greenwood spirit, Marian was not prepared for the overwhelming, unearthly beauty of the babe in her arms.

The baby's skin was a warm golden colour and glistening with new life, like a leaf covered with early morning dew. The matted tuft of hair on the crown of her head was golden too, like honey. She appeared almost human but not quite. Not less than human, but more. The tips of her ears were ever so slightly pointed, like the elves of the forest, and she glowed with a magical energy. A physical body imbued with the life force of an immortal. The tiny girl gripped Marian's finger with her chubby hand and opened her eyes.

Her ever-weakening heart overflowing with love, Marion let out a shallow gasp as she saw the eyes that looked up at her. Large, wide and brown like her own, dancing with light, life and magic. The baby gurgled and Marian closed her eyes. She smiled serenely as her spirit left her body.

Leaning over, Robin brushed the hair from his lover's face and kissed her on the forehead. A kiss of pure love but a kiss that neither of them could feel.

Gently, Robin lifted the little girl from Marian's arms and held her to his chest. His heart swelled with love but it was a love tinged with sadness because he knew that, in the brief moment that Marian had held their daughter, felt the warmth of her tiny body against her own, they had experienced a closeness that he could never share. The bond between a mortal parent and their child.

Daughter of the Forest

Squeezing the water from her hair, Holly looked at her reflection in the rippling stream. She had seen the mortal girls as they walked to the market, gathered flowers or played in the forest. Like her father, Holly could make her form invisible to mortal eyes, enabling her to watch the world of the mortals without being observed, but she longed for more. She longed to know what it meant to be human.

She had watched the children who played in the forest as they revelled in their games and adventures of their own creation, lost in each other's company and their own imagination. She missed the feeling of being a child like any other, being part of the mortal world.

A being unlike any other, Holly had been born in the forest, the daughter of an immortal spirit and a mortal woman. Her father was the great guardian spirit of the greenwood, Robin of the Wood, and her mother the only woman he had ever loved, Marian. Many in the forest referred to her as a wood nymph but in truth this was simply an assumed term for convenience. There was no word to describe what Holly truly was.

For the first ten summers of her life she had been cared for and protected by an elderly mortal lady to whom Robin had entrusted her as a newborn infant but now she was gone, severing the last link Holly had with the mortal world, bringing her completely into the world her Father and the other spirits of the forest inhabited.

She looked at her face reflected up at her in the water. He skin had a warm, golden colour as did her hair, warm like the light of the sun which shone down between the branches of the trees. Her eyes, like her mother's, were large and brown. The tips of her ears were ever so slightly pointed but she was sure that, if she let her hair hang loose, they would be covered. She knew that most mortals chose not to see things which they couldn't understand so she was fairly certain that she could pass for one of them.

Climbing out of the water, Holly stretched herself out on a wide, flat rock to let the sun dry her shimmering body. She closed her eyes and listened to the birds singing in the trees above her, enjoying the warm caress of the sun on her skin.

She was roused from her meditation by the voices of two girls, chattering happily as they strolled along the path through the forest. Quick as a flash, Holly disappeared, blending her form against the rock, as the girls sauntered down to the water.

The two little peasants kicked off their simple sandals and sat at the edge of the stream, dabbling their feet in the warm, gently flowing water. Holly watched them as she had done so many times before. She thought for only a moment before making her decision, the decision to leave her world behind and enter the mortal world.

She dived into the water, lifting the veil of invisibility with which she had concealed herself. The girls, thinking that they were alone, were shocked when Holly emerged in front of them, blowing water in their faces. Their alarm lasted for only a few seconds then they laughed and splashed her with their feet.

Pulling herself up out of the stream, Holly sat beside them.

"Hello," she said. "What brings you two down here?"

"We're on our way to the market to get some meat and flour", the first girl replied. "What about you?"

"Oh, I live here!" she told her. The girl looked surprised.

"In the forest?" she enquired, looking rather incredulous. Holly realised her mistake and quickly corrected herself.

"Well, near here anyway. A cottage at the edge of the forest. I live with my cousins. My name's Holly."

"Ysabel," the girl introduced herself, "and this is my sister Claire."
For a time, all three sat dabbling their feet in the water, enjoying the warm sunshine. After a while, Claire looked at Holly with curiosity.

"Where are your clothes?" she asked.

Feigning surprise, Holly looked around as if she expected to see them in a bundle nearby.

"Oh I expect one of the others pinched them while I was swimming. It's their rather feeble idea of a joke! But I suppose I can't go into the village like this." She grinned rather sheepishly. "I don't suppose either of you could lend me something could you?"

Giggling, Claire handed Holly the travelling cloak she had been carrying over her arm, in case it got colder once the sun went in and Ysabel gave her the large square of cloth she was carrying to wrap their purchases in. Wrapped around and tied at one shoulder, it made a reasonable tunic. Holly swung the cloak around her shoulders. Beautifully woven dark green wool which hung past her knees, and a hood. A hooded cloak for the daughter of the hooded man, she thought to herself.

"I suppose," Ysabel said, nodding towards the path which led to the village, "If we're going to get there before everything's gone we'd better get going!"

All three girls headed down the path through the forest, talking merrily as they went. Holly even taught them some of the songs of the forest folk and the sisters taught her some of their own favourites, the ones their grandmother had taught to them before she died.

By and by, they emerged from the forest into the open. A small inn stood at the edge of the woods, a horse cart lying broken and abandoned outside. Not too far in the distance, the girls could see the first huts and dwellings of the village. They pressed onwards.

Shivering, Holly pulled the borrowed cloak tighter around her shoulders. This was the first time in her life she had ventured beyond the boundaries of the forest and it frightened her. Her guardian had never taken her to the village or anywhere outside of the forest, at the insistence of her father. There had been mortal visitors to the cottage, friends and family, who had brought with them wonderful tales and explanations of the world outside but Holly had never seen it for herself. Her only contact with mortals had been those who came to her. They had been in her world. Now, for the first time, she was in their world, dressed like one of them and walking amongst them. Holly felt cold, despite the warmth of the sun above them, and pulled the cloak tighter around her shoulders. They reached the market.

The sights, sounds and smells were overpowering. Well-fed merchants presided over lavish displays laid out on sturdy oaken trestles while peasant farmers hawked their meagre wares from trays slung around their neck. People from all walks of life bustled together in the throng. Servants from the castle bought provisions for the feasts and poor women bought what little food they could afford for their family while their ragged children played in the mud with the dogs who eagerly snapped up any choice morsels which happened to fall to the floor.

A dark-skinned man in a blue robe sold exquisite jewellery from a mat spread out on the ground, the baker and the grocer shouted to advertise their wares and a large man with a red face offered the customers sips of his whisky in the hope of enticing them to buy a bottle or two.

On a platform in the centre of the market square stood a tall, brightly dressed man. His black hair was tied back with a red ribbon and he held a rather battered lute which looked like it could have been older than him – passed down to him by his father perhaps, or even his grandfather.

"Gather round! Gather round!" he cried. "And I shall tell you the tales of bold Robin Hood!"

Holly smiled. Her father had told her that the mortals liked to tell stories of his exploits. Stories which became more and more fanciful with each retelling. As a small crowd started to encircle the minstrel, he continued:

"Gather round and I shall tell you of his adventures in the Greenwood. How he fought against evil, robbed from the rich to feed the poor and won the heart of the fair Lady Marian!"

At the sound of her mother's name, Holly felt a twinge of sadness. She had never known her but she saw the look in her father's eyes when he talked about her, and when he told her how fragile and precious mortal life was. Her mother may not have had many years but she lived each of those years, each moment, to the full. Her father often said that in twenty years she had lived more than many people would if they lived to be a thousand. She wished she could have met her, seen those beautiful brown eyes she was told were so like hers. A tear formed in the corner of her eye. She brushed it away and turned to look for her new friends.

She found them talking to the blacksmith, watching him as he hammered out the blade of a new sword fit for a knight. The white glow from the furnace hurt her eyes and she felt even colder. The girls greeted her and she tried to smile at them but found herself shaking uncontrollably. She dropped to her knees. The sisters rushed to her side and the blacksmith downed his tools to assist her.

He lifted her head with a hand which, though rough and calloused, was surprisingly gentle. He pulled back the hood which had flopped forward, concealing her face and looked at her intently, his eyes full of concern.

"My poor child", he said, soothingly, "You've been struck by a fever. We must find you somewhere to rest." He turned to Ysabel and Claire. "Do you know who she is?" he asked. "Where does she live?"

The girls explained how they had met Holly in the forest. They didn't know exactly where she lived but they were fairly sure it was on the other side of the forest.

"Well she can't walk, poor thing." He said, beckoning to a boy of about fifteen, his apprentice, to come and take over the forge. "My wife can care for her until she's well enough to be taken home."

He lifted Holly up effortlessly and carried her into the hut behind the forge where he and his wife lived when his work was not taking him to the big towns as it sometimes did for months at a time.

Her matted hair plastered to her face, Holly dripped with sweat. Her eyes, normally so vibrant and full of energy were dull and bloodshot. The blacksmith carried her inside and laid her down on the straw matting which served as their bed.

"Poor lamb! Whatever is the matter with her?" cried the blacksmith's wife, a kind-faced, matronly woman with greying brown hair tied up in a bun at the back of her head.

"She collapsed in the square," her husband explained, the two sisters pushing through the doorway behind him to check on their new friend. "She's gripped by fever!"

The girls squatted down beside the mat and held Holly's hands as the blacksmith's wife dipped a rag in a bucket of cold water and placed it gently across her forehead. She then hurried over to the stove and started chopping herbs which she threw into a large pot and began to boil.

Feeling weak and nauseous, Holly was terrified. She had never known anything like it. Wood nymphs don't get sick, or at least that's what she had believed until now. She felt the girls beside her but when she tried to look at them her vision was blurred and the light made her eyes sting. She felt the woman come over and pour a spoonful of some strange tincture down her throat. The taste was not unpleasant but it did nothing to alleviate the terrible burning in her head or the shivering.

She could hear the blacksmith and the others talking but she could not hear what they said, not that she cared any more. The pain she felt was terrible and she didn't understand why. She felt the cold compress on her forehead replaced with a different one, warm this time with a slightly sickly scent like some of the berries in the forest. The forest. Her forest. Her home.

She began to thrash around on the mat. They wrapped her in blankets to stop her injuring herself and looked on in desperation as the poor child struggled for breath. She took two very deep breaths and opened her eyes. The spark had gone from them. They knew that she was dead. The blacksmith closed her eyes and said a simple prayer before covering her face with one of the blankets. The girls began to cry. He put his big arms round them to comfort them while his wife went to fetch the priest and carpenter.

All at once the pain was gone. Holly found herself in a forest, but it was not the forest she knew. The whole place was bathed in a warm green light and a crystal clear stream tickled happily between rocks of warm, red granite. She looked around at the trees. Not one of them was dead or damaged, there were no withered or broken branches or rotted leaves. The birds and squirrels in the trees were all healthy and well fed.

Suddenly, Holly realised that she was not alone. Sitting on one of the rocks, dabbling her feet in the crystal water, was a young woman. She was sure that she had never seen her before but at the same time she looked strangely familiar.

The woman turned towards her and smiled. Her big brown eyes twinkled, reflecting the shimmering water. Holly knew who she was.

Although she had never seen her before, she knew deep in her heart that this was her mother. She ran towards her, leaping over the rocks and splashing through the stream to get to this mysterious woman who all at once was both a stranger and a lifelong friend.

The two flung their arms around each other. It was as if they had never been separated, as if the fourteen years that Holly had spent without her mother were insignificant moments. It didn't matter that they had been apart for so long. What mattered was that they were together now.

The joy of the reunion was marred ever so slightly when a troubling thought came to Holly's mind.

"Am I dead?" She asked.

"For the moment," her mother replied, looking in her eyes and giving her a reassuring smile. "But your father is immortal, you are a daughter of the forest. Like the trees which lose their leaves in the autumn, only to be covered with blossom in the spring, or the plants which die back to the ground when the frosts come, you will rise up again under the sun, re-energised and stronger than you ever were before."

"But why did I die?" asked the child, returning her mother's steady gaze.

"If a tree is cut down, or a flower pulled away from its roots, it will die." Explained Marian in a steady, soothing voice. "A child of the forest cannot live outside of it. When you left your world it was as if your roots had been cut. You could not live."

Another thought slipped quietly into Holly's head. She turned her face away from Marian's smile and looked down into the water. Her reflection looked back at her, sad and reproachful.

"What's the matter, my darling?" asked Marian, concerned by her daughter's sudden sadness. She ran her fingers gently through her golden hair. Holly turned to look at her, tears welling up in her big brown eyes.

"It's my fault that you're dead." She said quietly. "I know that you died giving birth to me. If it wasn't for me you'd still be alive!"

"No, my darling, no. That's not true. I died because it was my time to die. It wasn't because of anything you or anyone else did. You mustn't ever think that it was your fault!"

"But if you had never had me then you might still be in the forest, with my father. You could still be alive!"

"Do I look like I'm dead now?" asked Marian, gently, smiling once more at her daughter. "It's true that I left my mortal body behind, like so many have done before and will continue to do until the end of time. But my immortal soul, the part of all of us that makes us who we are, will live forever."

Marian looked wistfully into the distance.

"I miss your father terribly," she said quietly, "but the time I spent with him was wonderful. Many people's mortal lives drag on for years and when they reach the end they realise that they have not truly lived a single day. The months I spent with Robin were worth a thousand lifetimes and our love lives on in you. My beautiful, immortal daughter. You are the best of both of us because you were born from love. True love. Love so deep that words could never describe it."

"But now you're separated from him eternally! He is immortal and can never die so you will be apart forever!"

"Not forever, my child. Just for a while. Like spring follows the winter and life returns to the dead plants, the world of death will pass away. A time will come when the mortal world and the immortal will be as one. There will be no more death, or suffering or fear and we will all be together for eternity. We will be a family once more as we were always meant to be."

"When will that day come? It could be years, centuries, thousands of years! Must we be apart so long?"

Taking her daughter's face in her hands, Marian studied her features with fascination. She looked so like she had as a child, yet also like her father – brave, honest and wise. She kissed her tenderly on the forehead.

"When you arrived here, did you know who I was?"

"Well, yes I did. I felt like I recognised you somehow."

"And have you seen me before? Do you remember me from when you were born?"

"No, I don't think so." Holly furrowed her brow. "I'd always tried to imagine what you might look like when father talked about you but I'm sure I've never actually seen you before I arrived here."

"And when did you arrive here?"

Thinking hard, Holly realised that she really couldn't be sure. Part of her knew that she had been with the other girls at the market less than an hour ago, yet another part of her thought she had been in this magical forest much longer – years, or even centuries. Her life before was starting to feel like a half-forgotten dream, almost as if she had always been there forever.

"I don't know," she confessed. "It feels like I've always been here."

"And that's what it will be like then." Marian told her. "However long we have to wait before we're together again, once we are it will feel like we've never been apart. We'll know everyone and be together forever. Mortal and immortal, there will be no difference. We will all be together."

"I don't want to wait though," cried Holly, tears rolling down her cheeks, "I want to stay. I want to stay with you!"

Putting her arms around her daughter, Marian held her tight. She stroked her hair soothingly.

"I'm always with you. I'm a part of you and you live in my heart. It's not your time yet. Your season has not yet passed. You must return to the world you came from. Rejoin your father."

She looked down into the water. The reflection had changed slightly. It was less clear, less perfect, yet more fragile and beautiful.

"My life was precious because it was so short. I lived every day knowing that tomorrow may not come so every day must be lived to the full and enjoyed as if it were my last. But you are immortal. You will live with your father until the end of time when the mortal world comes to an end. Think of what you can do, what you can see. You can make plans and see ventures through to the end because you always know there will be a day after."

"It seems so cruel," Holly sobbed. "That I should be shown this place but not allowed to stay. Thrown out of paradise."

"But you have seen it." Marian said, cradling her weeping daughter in her arms. "So you will always know that it is here. You have seen me. You know that I am immortal like you and one day we will be reunited. No one can ever take that knowledge from you, so you need never fear the future and what is to come."

Staring into the water again, Marian thought of her lost love, of Robin.

"Your father knows of this place but he has never seen it. He can only have faith that it is as he has been told, but you know. You know for certain. You have been given a wonderful gift. To die and be able to go back. To tell those you love that there is nothing to fear beyond the boundaries of the mortal realm, and that is why you must go back."

"Must I go now?" asked Holly, looking at the strange distorted reflection in the stream.

"Yes my daring", Marian replied tenderly. Time moves differently here to the mortal world. We have been together here less than an hour but in the world you came from the summer has passed. Frost has covered the ground and the trees are bare but now the frost has begun to melt, the sun shines bright in the sky and soon the branches of the trees will be covered with blossom. It is time for you to be reborn."

"Come with me!" pleaded Holly. "Come back to the mortal world. Live again!"

"I cannot." Marian told her, kindly but firmly. "I have had my season. I was a mortal in the mortal world and now I have left it. My time has passed. But you are a daughter of the forest, an immortal in the mortal world. You must go back and you must live."

"But how do I get back?" Holly asked. "I don't know how! I don't know the way!"

Taking her daughter's hand in one of her own and leading her to the side of the pool, Marian waved her other towards the water. Together they looked at the reflection. Holly realised that it was not the forest she sat in reflected but rather the world from which she had come, viewed through the rippling stream.

"Dive in." She said. "Your world is beyond the water. Leave this world and go back to your own. Return to the mortal world. Live!"

Both stood on the rock on which they had been sitting. They shared a final kiss. Holly stretched out her arms, bent her knees and plunged into the crystal water.

The village priest repeated the well-worn liturgy over the simple wooden coffin. The blacksmith took the lid from where it rested against the wall and laid it in place, covering Holly's lifeless body. Reverently as he knew how, he hammered in the nails in place to seal the coffin.

No one knew who the mysterious girl was. No one had seen her before or knew her family. The sisters went to look for the cottage at the edge of the woods where they had first met Holly, where she had told them she lived, but they found no such home. She seemed to have come from nowhere.

Finally it was decided that she should be buried in the forest. That was where she had come from and, for all anyone knew, where she lived, alone and wild.

A small procession of the blacksmith and his wife, the sisters with their parents and the priest walked quietly along the path into the forest, the coffin born on the shoulders of the blacksmith and the sister's father. They came to a clearing beneath a wide, leafy oak tree and the two younger men dug a hole while the priest led prayers and the women and girls sung hymns and songs of mourning.

The coffin was lowered into the ground and covered over with rich, fertile soil. Claire and Ysabel planted a single white rose to mark the site of the grave then they all returned to their homes and their lives.

Beneath the tree in the forest, the petals of the rose turned brown and fell to the ground where they mingled with the leaves fallen from the branches of the oak above. Small creatures scurried around, living in and from the decaying leaves as they became mulch to fertilise the next generation of plants on the forest floor. The trees all around became bare. Dead. The rose looked like nothing more than a lifeless stick casually thrust into the earth. Frost covered the branches above and turned the ground as hard as stone.

Slowly, almost imperceptibly, the ground began to soften. The sun shone for longer, higher in the sky. Drips of pure water fell from the tips of branches and the first plants of spring, dormant for so long, began to push their way up through the thawing soil, relishing the strength and nourishment they drew from the remains of those who had come before, those plants and small animals whose seasons had passed.

The sun shone high in the sky. Green leaves appeared on the stem of the rose. New growth stretched out towards the sky and buds formed which blossomed forth into beautiful flowers.

Down and down Holly swam into the warm, clear water. Ever further she pushed but never touched the bed. Gradually she realised that she was no longer heading down, now she was swimming upwards, towards the light. She felt a rush of energy unlike anything she had ever felt before as she burst through the surface of the water to feel the warm summer sun on her face. She was alive. A wood nymph, stripped of the last vestiges of the mortal world she had so briefly experienced, she was immortal once more. She knelt in front of the rose, holding the sweet-smelling flower gently in her hands. Her father stood behind her and placed a hand of her shoulder.

"I've missed you." He told her, simply but sincerely. "We all have."

Smiling up at him, Holly knew that she was home, where she belonged. Eve in her own paradise. A daughter of the forest.

After a good many days, the flood-waters had begun to subside. Holly picked her way carefully through the mud, between the dark puddles which still filled the hollows and dips on the forest floor.

Many of the plants and ferns which carpeted the forest were still curled protectively, sheltering from the water which had covered them until the night before. The aftermath of the flood was most evident around the beautiful lakes, fed by underground springs.

A powerful rotting smell emanated from the mess of dead fish and water plants which the flood-waters had deposited around the banks when they receded. Holly covered her nose and looked away, hoping not to tread in any of the foetid mush.

As she looked around her, Holly became aware of a noise. Only a small noise, such as a wounded animal might make. Somewhere between a whimper and a sob. Holly searched for the source of the noise, thinking that some small creature may have been trapped or injured by the flood and the damage it caused.

It did not take Holly long to locate where the sound originated.

It was coming from a figure sat huddled at the bottom of a tree. At first, Holly thought that it might be one of the human children from the village who had lost her way in the woods, but the sound was not quite human.

Gingerly, Holly approached the figure and knelt down beside them. The figure was that of a girl, huddled under the tree with her knees drawn up under her chin. Holly noticed with a start that the girl's ears were slightly pointed, like her own. Holly reckoned her age to be one or two years less than she herself appeared. Her black hair was impossibly long and matted, wrapped all around her body. The hair itself had a slight greenish sheen, like the algae which clings to a rock at the bottom of a pond.

Having reached out to touch the girl on the arm, Holly drew her hand back in alarm. The girl's skin, as well as being so pale it was almost white, was ice cold and clammy as if the girl's body was riddled with fever.

The girl turned her head towards Holly who saw that her eyes were large, wider even than her own which were rather wider than those of an average human, and a very pale, ice blue colour.

"What's your name?" asked Holly. The girl looked back at Holly blankly, clearly not understanding the question.

"Where are you from?" Holly tried again, "Where's your home?"

The girl's eyes narrowed a little.

"Home." She repeated.

"Home." Holly confirmed. "Where is home?"

"Home." The girl simply repeated the word once more, apparently attracted by its sound rather than any recognition.

"Come on," said Holly, taking charge of the situation, "You can't stay here. Let's get you somewhere safe."

Narrowly avoiding slipping in the mud, Holly helped the girl to her feet and they were just starting along the rather squishy path when Holly heard voices in the distance. They seemed to be getting closer.

"Quick!" she said, tugging on the girl's arm. "We need to get out of sight!"

At Holly's insistence, the girl followed her into the undergrowth and squatted down beside her, just out of sight of any passing travellers.

"We'll wait here until they've passed," Holly whispered. She knew the girl could not understand her words, but her voice was soothing and she hoped to keep the girl calm, "then we'll go and find my father. He'll know what to do!"

Two women were approaching along the path, picking their way carefully through the puddles and putrefying deposits, probably on their way to the market for the first time since the floods had hit twelve days ago.

Crouching fearfully, Holly waited for them to pass. She knew, if necessary, she could blend her appearance with the forest around her so as not to be seen, but she had no guarantee that this girl could do the same.

Suddenly, and without warning, the girl sprang to her feet and ran towards the women. Holly reached out to stop her but the girl was too quick.

The women gasped as the pale, naked child sprang onto the path in front of them. She crouched on the ground, like a cat about to spring, and fixed them with a wide-eyed stare.

"Home" she cried. "Home! Home!"

Overcoming their shock, the women both knelt down in front of her. One placed her hands gently on the shoulders of the girl, who had begun to shiver despite the warmth of the air. Although her face registered surprise, she did not pull back when she touched the girl's clammy skin.

"Are you lost?" She asked, softly.

Listening from the undergrowth, Holly was relieved to hear the kindness in the woman's voice.

"Home." The girl repeated.

The other woman stood and unfastened her cloak, which she wrapped around the girl's shoulders. Taking an arm each, they gently raised her to her feet. At first the girl resisted but she seemed to sense that the women meant her no harm.

"You don't look well," Said the first woman, "we need to get you something good to eat, then we can find out where you come from."

"Home."

"Yes," the second woman smiled sweetly, bending slightly to tenderly kiss the top of the girl's matted head, "We'll get you home."

Unable to do anything, Holly could only watch helplessly as they led the girl away towards the village. She knew in her heart that the women were kind and would take care of her, but she did not know how long this strange girl could survive in the world of humans. She vowed at that moment that she would keep watch as best she could and see that no harm befell the girl.

The women who had found her were sisters. One was the wife of the village blacksmith and had three young children, two girls and a boy, so she took the girl into raise alongside her own.

The girl was unable to speak to tell them her name, so her adoptive parents chose one for her. Remembering the legends they had heard during their own childhood about mysterious women who appeared from the water, they named her Elkie.

As the months passed, Elkie began to look more and more human. Her skin lost its cold, bluish pallor, leaving her looking pale but healthy, her white skin making an attractive contrast to her jet black hair, now clean, flowing and devoid of any trace of the green tint it had once held. Even her ears seemed to have lost their unusual shape and were now gently curved like those of any other girl in the village.

It was not long before Elkie began to speak. She was a fast learner and apparently a natural mimic, picking up the language spoken by those around her remarkably fast. Within a year she could converse fluently and there was very little to make her stand out from the other village children, apart from her piercing, ice blue eyes.

What was perhaps more surprising to Holly, who often sat in the branches of the trees at the edge of the village, watching this strange visitor, was that Elkie appeared to be ageing normally. So alike had they been when Holly found her that she had expected Elkie to remain eternally young like herself but, Holly reflected, Elkie had never died.

As the months turned into years, Elkie grew into a beautiful young woman, not only catching they eyes of village boys but turning heads from far and wide with her exotic, ethereal beauty when she visited the market with her adoptive family.

On the first Monday of every month, Holly would watch Elkie as she walked through the forest on her way to the market, accompanied at first by her father, and later, as they all got older, by her brothers and sisters. Holly kept to the shadowy branches high up in the trees, not wanting to alarm the mortals, but one day she saw that Elkie was alone so she took the opportunity to speak to her.

Springing gracefully down from the overhead bows, Holly landed at Elkie's side and greeted her with a smile. Elkie gasped as she recognised Holly.

"You're the girl who helped me!" she exclaimed. "But you haven't changed at all! You look exactly the same!"

"Hmm. I do have that tendency." Holly smiled. "My name's Holly."

"They call me Elkie,"

"I know," Holly said, smiling cheekily, "I've heard!"

"How did you...?"

Shrugging, Holly tried to look innocent. Then she grinned widely and admitted the truth.

"I've been keeping an eye on you since you went to the village."

"Then I suppose you don't need to be told my news?" asked Elkie, smiling coyly. Holly was greatly intrigued.

"What news?"

"Well," said Elkie, biting her bottom lip nervously, "I'm getting married!"

"Married?" exclaimed Holly with delight.

"Yes. A young man from the next village has asked me to be his wife and I've said yes! We're to be married next month!"

"That's fantastic!" said Holly, flinging her arms around her friend as the two of them bounced up and down with excitement. "I wish I could come," she continued, a tinge of sadness in her voice, "but I can't leave the forest."

Just for a moment, Elkie looked sad but then her face brightened as she realised that her wedding procession would have to pass through the forest on their way to the chapel in her future husband's village. Holly promised that she would be there to wave to Elkie as they passed.

Standing back for a moment, Holly looked thoughtful. Then she asked the question she had been burning to ask throughout the whole encounter.

"You never did tell me where you came from?"

Briefly, Elkie looked away, her vivid blue eyes somehow distant. She turned back To Holly.

"From the world below." She said quietly.

Holly was puzzled.

"The world below?"

"Beneath the water. A beautiful kingdom of goodness and light." A single tear formed in the corner of her eye. "The priests in the village told me of this world, how it was once perfect but fell from that perfection. My world did not fall. My world is paradise."

Although shorter than her friend, Holly wrapped her arms tenderly around Elkie's neck and held her close. She looked up into her large, round eyes and saw the sadness of loss they held.

"Why did you stay? Why did you not go back?"

"When you found me I was crying," Elkie reminisced, "I had been trying for hours to return, but whenever I jumped into the water, all I found was the bottom of the lake. The gateway to my world was closed."

"Then how...?"

"I was pushed through with the flood-water, and when the waters subsided the gateway disappeared with them and I was trapped."

All of a sudden, her face brightened up and her voice lifted.

"But," she continued, "I have a new life here, and soon it's going to get even more exciting. Not very long from now I'll have a family of my own!"

They hugged once more and Elkie went to continue on her way, pausing only to extract a further promise from Holly that she would be there to wave as her wedding procession passed through the forest.

The day of the wedding came soon enough and Holly stood, with her father, John, Ket and Hob, to wave to her friend as she passed. Elkie waved back and Holly thought her heart would burst with joy. She blew a kiss then faded back into the forest.

The seasons continued to pass and Holly watched as Elkie and her husband were blessed first with a son then, a little less than two years later, twin daughters. The children were human of course, but retained a great deal of their mother's ethereal beauty, which was remarked upon by all who came across them.

Often, Elkie would walk with her children in the forest. On one such occasion, they came across a stream, running with clear, pure water. As children are inclined to do, they pulled off their shoes and leapt into paddle.

At the sight of the water, Elkie felt a pang of homesickness, but her children looked so happy and natural in the water that she could not bring herself to begrudge them their play.

Sitting on the ground, Elkie dabbled her feet in the water while she watched her three children playing and splashing happily in the stream. Her face was smiling but her eyes betrayed a distant, wistful expression.

For a moment, it seemed like her mind was far away. Then her son splashed her playfully, making her laugh and splash him back so he shrieked with happiness. Elkie stood and waded her way into the middle of the shallow stream and joined in the game. It was not long before she slipped and ended up sitting in the water with the children, her dress was soaked but she didn't care! She was just happy to be in the water.

More than thirty summers passed and Elkie's children grew, married and had children of their own. As mortal men all must, her husband died, quietly in his bed from a fever, yet Elkie continued to walk in the forest.

As time passed, Holly would walk with her, listening to her friend's stories of life in the mortal world, and sharing with her the tales of the forest. Then one day, the floods returned.

Elkie looked out across the water.

She and Holly had splashed their way through the shallows, stopping every now and then to remove the trailing weeds which got caught around their feet. They stood on a small hillock, which rose above the flood-water Holly knew what her friend was thinking.

"It's been forty summers." said Elkie, thoughtfully. "Almost an entire mortal lifetime."

Gently, Holly put her hand on Elkie's shoulder.

"Do you think…" Elkie broke off, composed herself a little then spoke again, "Is there a chance? Could the gateway to my world be open once more?"

Instinctively, in her being, Holly knew that it was true. She could sense the waters rippling with that indefinable energy which mortals called magic.

"If it's what you want," she said, rather slowly, "then you can return. But it must be today. Right now. There may never be another chance in your lifetime."

Turning, Elkie saw the sadness in her friend's eyes.

"You've been a true friend to me." She said gently. "You found me, looked after me. You've been my guardian and companion all these years. But look at you. Still a beautiful child, while I grow ever older."

Her eyes stinging, Holly struggled to fight back the tears. She knew it was right for Elkie to return to her home, to her people, but they had been friends for so long.

"My children are grown," Elkie continued. "They have no further need of me, and my husband is gone. If I remained here, in no more than another ten summers I would be gone too. And you would remain, exactly as you are now."

Holding her friend's hands, Holly spoke quietly and gently to her.

"I may never become any older," she began, "and my body may never grow, but my heart does. I've lived for over fifty summers, and for forty of those you have been my friend. As I've watched you grow, becoming a woman and experiencing the joy of being a mother, it has helped me to grow too."

She pulled one of Elkie's hands towards her so that it rested over her heart.

"Your friendship, your love, has helped me to grow. I can never experience the life of a mortal, but you have allowed me to share in the joy of yours. My appearance may not have changed but we have grown together."

She released Elkie's hands and smiled warmly.

"Now, don't miss your chance! You've had an adventure in my world, who knows what still awaits you in your own?"

Elkie flung her arms around Holly.

"I'll never forget you!" she said, with a smile of pure love.

Then she turned, faced the water, lifted her arms above her head and dived.

As Elkie leapt into the water, it was as if the last forty years had ever existed. She was a girl once more. Her long black hair, now tinged with green as it had been so many years before, formed a billowing cloud around her as she broke back up through the surface.

Without saying a word, she beckoned to Holly, who dove in after her. Hand in hand, they plunged deeper and deeper. Holly had returned from another world through the water before, but this felt different.

They swam deeper and deeper and slowly, almost imperceptibly at first, the warm orange light from the sun above was replaced by a different light, a cool, blue light from below. Down and down they swam, the light becoming brighter all the time.

All of a sudden, Holly saw something which almost took her breath away. It was an entire city, larger than any settlement she had seen on the land, far larger than Nottingham or even London, and seemed to be constructed entirely from pale blue crystals which shimmered in the light which seemed to radiate from the heart of the tallest building in the underwater metropolis, a castle – no, a palace, it's twisting spires reaching up towards the surface.

There were no streets in this world. The citizens, all pale and ethereal like Elkie, water beings in their unspoilt world so unlike the fallen world of the surface, swam around each other, entering the buildings and their homes at any level. Fantastic aquatic beasts swirled around in the joyful throng with the water folk. It was a perfect world. A peaceful world. But not Holly's world.

With a pang of pain, Holly realised that she could not stay. This was not where she belonged. She would be as much of an outsider here, as totally alone, as Elkie had been in her world. Facing her friend and slowly peddling the water beneath her while she held her hands, Holly gave Elkie a soft kiss of farewell and pushed upwards, leaving the tranquil blue world beneath her as she returned to her own spoiled but warm and green forest in the world on the surface.

For as long as he could remember, Robert had loved the forest. As a little boy he used to play there, climbing the trees and sitting very quietly in the hope of spotting some of the wild rabbits and other timid creatures that lived in the undergrowth.

He knew all the stories the people told of the fantastical beings that were supposed to inhabit the greenwood – immortal spirits from a realm between this world and the next. He knew of John o'the stumps, the gentle giant who protected the trees. He knew of the brothers, Ket and Hob, the watchers, troll-like little men who saw all and knew everything that went on in the forest. And he knew about Robin.

He had first heard the stories from his grandfather, the Earl of Loxley. In those first years after his parents died, taken by a plague which had swept through the villages like an angel of death – claiming the lives of many and forcing more to abandon their homes, fleeing to the forest or even to the sea to escape it's ravages, they had sat by the fire each evening and Grandfather had told him magical tales of the woodland folk. Robert had been captivated by all of them, but his favourite were the tales of the hooded man – Robin of the Wood. A great hero and guardian of the forest. Charged forever to defend humanity against all the forces the powers of evil could muster.

Young Robert had been thrilled by these stories and the tales of the great adventures that Robin and his friends led in the forest. When he played there he would imagine that he himself was the mystical archer. He imagined himself fighting for justice against the forces of darkness.

As he grew, the young man would enjoy walking in the quiet woodland, the mighty oak trees with their ancient, passive wisdom giving him space to think and to contemplate. Sometimes he would sit for a time beneath one of these proud wooden monoliths and compose poetry.

The pain Robert felt for the loss of his parents served to help him appreciate all the more the life that he had. He had a home, loving grandparents, food to eat and clothes to wear and, of course, the beauty of Sherwood forest to inspire him.

His grandfather was a good Lord, as he himself pledged to be. The peasants and farmers who lived on his land all had food and their children were healthy, taxes were fair and rent could be accepted in kind, or postponed, indefinitely if needs be, if the household could not afford to pay.

Life was good.

Robert's grandfather had always been on good terms with the Sheriff of the Shire. He had fought alongside his father and was an old friend of the family, so Robert was not surprised to see the Sheriff riding up to the gates of Loxley Manor.

Returning from his walk in the forest, Robert saw the horses of the Sheriff and the two men who accompanied him. He climbed up into one of the apple trees that lined the path to get out of the way, unnoticed by the oncoming riders. He sat on a branch, munching an apple, and watched them pass.

As it was a warm autumn afternoon, he decided to stay in the tree for a while. Years of climbing the trees in the forest had given him excellent balance so he stretched himself out along the branch and closed his eyes, enjoying the sun's dappled warmth through the leaves and savouring the smell of the delicious ripe apples around him.

He wasn't sure if he had slept for hours or only minutes but it was still light when he was awoken by a sudden shriek from the direction of the Manor. He was about to jump down from the tree to investigate but stopped himself, instinctively, as the heavy oak doors burst open. The Sheriff's men came out first. Both had bodies slung across their shoulders. Robert's heart gave a sickening lurch when he recognised them as those of his grandparents. His grandmother had her throat cut and his grandfather's head was missing entirely. It took every ounce of self control Robert possessed not to cry out as the Sheriff followed his men out, laughing heartily and brandishing the Earl of Loxley's severed head. He watched in horror as the bodies were hung on gibbets and the head spiked on the end of a long spear which was stuck in the ground at the foot of the steps which led to the door. The Sheriff and his men returned inside, the Sheriff licking the blood from his hands as he went, and slammed the heavy doors shut with such force that the glass in the windows rattled.

Leaping down from his hiding place, Robert ran with all the speed he could muster into the forest; hot tears of grief and anger pouring down his cheeks, his heart racing and his brain burning with thoughts of vengeance. He ran and he ran through the forest he knew so well, the forest which he had considered a friend since his childhood. He ran until his legs could just not run any more then he slumped down beneath the wide spreading branches of an ancient oak tree and, physically and emotionally exhausted, fell into a deep, dreamless sleep.

As the first bright rays of morning penetrated the forest canopy, Robert awoke. At first he did not remember where he was or why, but all too quickly the sickening horror of the day before came flooding back to him. As well as the thoughts of revenge, his brain was troubled by many troubling questions – why had his grandfather been killed? Why, which was even harder to accept, by a man who he considered a friend, almost as close as family?

Sitting beneath the tree, Robert's mind churned with a thousand, confused thoughts. Suddenly, he became aware that he was not alone. A short, but very muscular little man, dressed in crudely tanned animal skins and no shoes, was watching him from the undergrowth. Robert sprang to his feet, alarmed and ready to defend himself against this strange observer, but the figure vanished into the bracken, hardly making a sound as he went.

"Don't be alarmed!" called a warm but commanding voice from behind him. "That's just Ket – he likes to keep and eye on what's going on! He's quite harmless but handy to have around!"

Spinning around, Robert found himself face to face with a tall man dressed in a green jerkin and cloak. His brown hair hung unkempt and windswept around his shoulders and his green eyes twinkled as he leant against the tree that Robert had been sitting against only moments before.

"Ket?" Robert exclaimed, "Not Ket the Trow, the watcher?"

"The very same!" replied the man, with a chuckle.

"Then you are...surely you can't be...?"

"Robin of the Wood, at your service." Announced the stranger, giving a sweeping bow to his new guest. Robert couldn't believe what he was hearing.

"The stories", he asked, "the tales my grandfather told me when I was a boy, they're all true?"

"Well I don't know about all of them," said a very large man, emerging from the tree. Robert blinked a few times and shook his head, unable quite to comprehend what he had just seen. The man had not walked round from behind the tree, or climbed out of a hollow in the trunk, he had stepped out of the tree. He had been a part of the tree yet had moved away from it and stood before Robert, solid and real as any other man he knew.

Yet this man was not like any other man he had ever seen. For a start he was incredibly tall, a good two foot taller than the tallest man Robert had encountered before, and solidly built. His hair, like Robin's, was brown but much coarser and Robert would not have been prepared to swear that it was not, in fact, made from very thin twigs. The leaves that seemed to have got tangled in his bushy mane, Robert realised with a jolt, were actually growing from it as if he were some strange hybrid of man and tree.

Despite his terrifying proportions, the giant had a good-natured manner about him and, after he'd taken a moment to get over the initial shock, Robert knew instinctively that he could trust him. The giant laughed at the look of incredulous surprise on Robert's face then smiled at him – a broad, toothy, reassuring smile.

"I'm known as John o'the stumps," the giant told him, "but my friends call me Little John. Anyway, as I was saying, I wouldn't say that all the stories they tell of us are true, but we're certainly real enough!"

Narrowing his eyes, Robin turned to Robert.

"I know." He said, his geniality of a moment before replaced by a grave solemnity. "I know why you fled. Why you sought sanctuary in our forest. The time will come when you will have to fight. When you must reclaim what is rightly yours. But for now you must survive."

At Robin's words, Robert felt the pain of the night before come flooding back, and tears pricked his eyes.

"How can I fight? How can I even survive? Where am I to go?"

"You will stay here with us", said Robin, in a tone which suggested that this was not an invitation but rather a command. "We will shelter you and we will teach you. But first, the Sheriff will come looking for you. If he hears that you are in the forest he will not rest until he has destroyed you. Robert of Loxley must disappear. He must die. From now on you will take my name."

He continued as Robert looked at him quizzically.

"My name is well known to the folk who live in the forest. The Sheriff knows the tales. If he hears of your activities he will just think they are talking about me and dismiss what he hears as peasant superstition. From now on, you shall bare my name. Robin. Robin Hood."

Autumn became winter and winter became spring. The leaves on the trees became brown and fell to the floor, to be replaced, in due time, by blossoms of pink and white and so life continued until the greenwood was green once more.

As the months and seasons passed, Robert made his home in the forest with the folk who had fled the plague which killed his parents or had no money to pay the increasingly cruel and oppressive taxes levelled by the Sheriff who had seized control of the Loxley estates after murdering their rightful lord.

He grew to know the ways of the forest. What in the past had been a place of recreation and relaxation became a home. He built a dwelling amongst the others from fallen wood, bark, leaves and mud. Learned to hunt, to cook and how to repair damaged clothing or fashion new garments from the remnants of others. He was accepted by the mortal forest-dwellers and became one of them.

Often at night, as they sat round the fire, the talk would turn to the immortals. The spirits of the forest and other non-human beings they shared their home with and their leader, Robin of the Wood, the hooded man. Each person had their story to tell, many of which grew more fantastical with each telling. Robert listened to these stories with a keen interest, knowing that with every day that passed the time was coming nearer when he would have to return to the world he had left to reclaim his rightful position.

Each day, as he worked, he could feel eyes watching him, the eyes of the forest. Robin and his fellow immortals knew all that happened in the forest. But sometimes it was different. Sometimes he felt as if there was someone else with him, by his side. It was not an alarming presence but friendly, as if he had an invisible companion. Sometimes he was sure that he heard giggling; a light, care-free, tinkling laugh, although it could simply have been the breeze whistling through the trees or a bird singing happily high in the branches. Robert felt sure that when the time was right this mysterious friend would make themselves known.

One day, he knew, Robin would come for him and his training would begin. He prayed that he would be equal to the challenge when the time came.

On the first day of the month of May Robert was gathering wood for the fire to cook his meal. A bundle of sticks in his arms, he bent down to pick up another. He was suddenly aware of a vast shadow looming over him. He swung round to see what terrible beast could cast such a spectre, dropping his sticks as he did so.

At first he was confused. What he found himself face to face with appeared to be a tree where there had been no tree moments before. Then he realised.

"John!" he cried, looking up into the face of the gentle giant high above him.

As John flashed his rough wooden teeth in a welcoming smile Robert was momentarily distracted by a woodlouse which seemed to be crawling out of John's ear, but his attention was soon drawn back when John spoke, simply but with resonance;

"It's time."

A Meeting of Hearts

Although he had always believed himself to be a competent archer, under Robin's tutelage Robert had excelled. Simply being able to shoot accurately would not be enough if he were to successfully lead the life of a greenwood outlaw, he must also learn how to fashion a bow and arrows from the wood available to him and how to fight effectively with a wooden staff, a hefty branch cut from a young tree, when required.

Through constant effort, dedication and practice, Robert learned many skills, not only from Robin and the other immortals but from the humans that Robin counted as allies, both those who lived wild in the forest and those in the villages to whom he was sent to learn the secrets of their unique abilities of combat and craftsmanship.

He devoted himself to his labours, pushing away thoughts of his murdered family and lost birthright as distractions which he must learn to avoid, or face the risk that his concentration may be fatally undermined when the critical moment came.

In the background, however, Robert was constantly aware of a strange presence. Not threatening in any way, more curious, as if someone, or something, were watching him from the shadows, trying to understand him. He had asked Robin what or who this observer may be but Robin had simply smiled in that engagingly enigmatic way of his and assured him that he had nothing to fear from "his little shadow", and that in time he was sure to discover more.

So it was that Robert began not only to trust his unseen companion but even to find their presence comforting and reassuring. In quiet moments, he even found himself talking to this strange phantom, addressing them as a friend although he received no reply.

In the summer nights, when the air was warm and the ground soft but dry, Robert loved to sleep in the open, the stars shining above him and a tree stump for his pillow. It was after a night such as this, as the sun's first warm, orange rays were creeping across the horizon, that Robert stirred, aware of a presence beside him.

Opening his eyes, Robert saw a figure sitting next to him, watching him as he slept. At first he took the observer to be a human girl, a normal child, but as his eyes adjusted he realised that this girl was far from normal.

Seeing his eyes open, she stood up, gasped and leapt up into the tree above. Robert looked up at her. Her large brown eyes were wide with anxiety.

Stretching out his hand towards the girl, Robert called out to her.

"It's okay, don't be afraid."

Shifting along the branch, the girl watched him warily. Robert realised suddenly that she was not frightened of him, rather she was fearful of scaring him away. He was sure that this was his little shadow of the past months.

Looking up to the tree, he gave an ostentatious bow.

"Robin Hood" he introduced himself, "at your service m'lady."

The girl giggled, a happy, tinkling sound that reminded Robert of a stream splashing its way over a pebble.

He smiled at her.

"And what, pray tell, is it that you find so funny?"

Apparently reassured by his good humour, the girl dropped down out of the tree. She stood in front of him, one hand on her hip and the other cupping her chin. She gave him an appraising look up and down.

"Well, you've got the cloak right but..."

"But?"

"I heard Robin Hood was a handsome man!"

The girl's eyes twinkled mischievously and Robert grinned back at her.

"Pardon me, fair lady, but I believe you have me at a disadvantage?"

The girl gave a bow even more sweeping and exaggerated that Robert's.

"Holly. I don't have any other names. At your service, naturally!"

"A delight to make your acquaintance." Said Robert, taking her hand and kissing it in a chivalrous fashion. "So," he continued, "I know your name but nothing else about you. What brings you to my forest kingdom?"

"You're forest kingdom?" enquired Holly, both hands on her hips and one eyebrow raised incredulously.

Dropping the air of mock-formality he had affected for their introduction, Robert plopped down onto a fallen log, patting the space by his side to invite Holly to join him. With a series of leaps and somersaults which would have taxed any human athlete to the absolute limit, Holly sprang across to the log and sat, cross-legged, beside Robert.

"Amazing!" Robert exclaimed, "You'll have to teach me how to do that!"

Holly snorted with mock derision.

"I think that may be a little beyond you, my fine fellow, but I'll gladly teach you as much as you can cope with!"

Hours passed as they sat there together, Holly explaining who she was and how she had been watching him since he was brought into the forest. She had been sure that she had seen him before, playing in the forest as a young boy, and she was fascinated to learn more about the man her father had chosen to bear his name.

The more she spoke, the more mesmerised Robert became by her vivid descriptions of the wonders of the forest, the mysterious worlds invisible to the mortal eye and the hidden worlds beyond. He thought he had seen most of the magic and the amazing creatures of the forest, but it was clear that he had seen but a tiny glimpse of all there was to see.

Of all the fantastic and mysterious beings he had met in the forest; Robin, John, Ket, Hob and so many others, it was this strangely fascinating wood nymph, a being far older than he as mortals measure time, with a wisdom far surpassing the wisest of men he had encountered in his life so far, yet in many ways so like a mortal child on the verge of womanhood, that he felt the strongest connection.

He had sensed the connection when she had been no more but an unseen presence. The feeling that he was not alone in facing the challenges that he would inevitably have to face. That someone would always be by his side, a loving friend and companion.

For her part, Holly had never met a man quite like Robert. Strong and brave yet with an unmistakeable look of sadness behind the twinkle in his eyes. In fact, never had she met a mortal man so like her immortal father. Yet it was not just that. Robert was unique, a being unlike any she had ever known. She felt drawn to him in a way she had never felt before. The feelings confused her. It somehow felt that she had been waiting her entire life to meet him. She made a pledge to herself that one day she would understand the nature of their bond, but until that time, she would stand by him, protect him and teach him what she could. When the time came for him to fight, as come it must, she would be sure that he was ready.

"I've been looking for you." Said Robin, not unkindly, "We need to talk."

Resting his bow against the tree, Robert turned to face his mentor. He had been wondering why Holly had made rushed excuses and vanished into the forest. He'd been worrying that he had unwittingly caused her some offence, but now he realised that she was keeping out of the way for this obviously important conversation.

"What is it?" He asked.

"Come," Robin gestured to a fallen log which he then sat upon, inviting Robert to join him. "There's some things you need to know."

"What things?"

"About the Sheriff who murdered your family. And about me."

Robert looked worried. He knew that all his training was building to the point where he could face the Sheriff and avenge his family, but it seemed now that there was more than he knew. He waited with baited breath to hear what Robin was about to tell him.

"Let me tell you a story," Robin began, "My story, like everyone's, begins with a mother and a father. The first mother and father in fact but unlike most mothers and fathers, these parents were not two but one. The Creator. She, I will call her she, lived alone in a beautiful garden she had created but she was lonely and longed for a companion to share the joy of existence with her. So, kneeling down on the soft grass, she dug some clay with her hands, worked and moulded it, sculpting lovingly, until she had created one like herself."

The story was familiar to Robert, he had been taught one much like it as a child but what, he wondered, could it have to do with the evil man who had betrayed and murdered his family. He allowed Robin to continue uninterrupted.

"She kissed the breath of life into him, I shall call him him as that is how he would later be known, but at the moment of his birth he was as his creator, a perfect blending of both mother and father, son and daughter. He awoke and looked with wonder at the beauty around him and for a time they were happy together, parent and child, in the beautiful, perfect garden. But this joy could not last. A creation can never be the equal of its creator. The man was as one with the garden, but not with his mother and he was lonely. The mother saw this and took pity upon him. She sent him into a deep sleep and while he slept she divided his nature in two, one man and one woman, so that both could be a companion for the other and neither would be lonely. It broke her heart to see her perfect creation split so but she knew it was the only way for her child, for her children to be happy. The man and the woman awoke, saw each other and knew instantly that each was the missing part of the other and that it was their destiny, their nature, to be together.

At first, they still walked with their mother in the garden, happy and joyful. Yet one day when the mother went to visit them she found that she was no longer welcome there and they did not want to see her. She did not know why and it broke her heart once more. She still walked in the garden, which began to grow and to cover the earth, but she stayed away from them and they from her. She longed to hold them close once more but when they heard her coming they would hide and, although she knew where they were even so, she would not force her presence or love upon them. If ever they returned to her, wanted her again, she would be ready to welcome them with open arms and an open heart but she knew she must wait for them to return in their own time."

"You're speaking of the Garden!" Robert interjected, "The man and his wife were cast out by the creator for their sin and disloyalty, not the other way around!"

"Do you really think," Robin smiled wistfully, "that a loving parent would set such a trap for their children as the familiar story tells? What is the one way," he asked Robert, "to guarantee that a child will touch something?"

"Tell them that they must not, under any circumstances, do so?" Robert answered. Nodding his head, Robin continued.

"Over time, when they looked back and could not understand why they had left Paradise behind, the children of the first man and woman created stories to explain it, casting the creator in the role of petulant, vengeful deity but, I ask again, could one filled with such love ever behave in such a way to their children?"

"No." Robert conceded, "They could not. But then why...?"

"I do not know." Robin admitted. "They simply grew away from their mother, wanting to achieve things by their own power rather than relying on her provision. It is the nature of humanity to be contrary. But if I may finish the story," Robin asked, "You may come to understand better." Robert nodded silently, allowing Robin to continue.

"And so," Robin explained, "time passed. Days became weeks, weeks became months and months became years. The man and the woman worked the land and grew food, refusing the free gifts offered by their mother, determined to survive on their own ability. The mother would gently help with their efforts, encouraging growth in the crops they planted and bringing rain to swell the fruits of their labours, but she never let them know of her involvement, allowing them to believe that what they had gained, they had gained on their own.

In due time, the man and woman were blessed with children of their own. Twin boys. They could not have looked more alike or been more different in temperament. One was kind, sociable, caring and wise. The other was mean, selfish, bad tempered and reclusive. The years continued to roll past and the man and woman were blessed with many more children, boys and girls. As time went on, the children grew, fell in love with one another and produced children of their own. The family lived together in peace and happiness, apart from the boy who had been born second of the first twins. He had grown into manhood, taken a wife and sired many children but still he was cruel and cold-hearted. He saw his brother's happiness and envied him. His own wife and children treated him with respect but kept a distance from him, afraid of his unpredictable rages and ill temper, yet his brother was beloved by all and his wife and children most of all."

Looking away, Robin fell silent for a few moments, as if reflecting on some deep hurt, an ancient wound which had yet to heal. The talk of families made Robert's eyes sting with tears as he remembered his own, destroyed both by disease and acts of unspeakable evil. He wanted to cry out, to ask what this had to do with his grandparents or the Sheriff but he kept silent, waiting for Robin to continue.

"The day came when he could contain his jealousy no more." Robin's voice cracked a little but he composed himself and continued. "He invited his brother to walk with him. They walked away from the family, away from the cultivated land and into the wilds of the garden. Out of sight, amongst the tall trees, he took a sharpened stone like the kind they used to create furrows for planting seeds in the earth and struck his brother a blow across the head. The innocent victim fell to the ground and instantly the life was gone from his body.

As the hapless victim's spirit left his body, there was a change over the entire garden. The sky became dark as night and howling winds tore through the trees, bringing many crashing to the ground and ripping the limbs from others. Animals yelped and howled in fear as they ran for their lives, others were not so lucky and were crushed by the falling wood. The ground beneath the murderer's feet became cold and hard, cracking and splitting as he ran. He ran onwards and onwards, away from the scene of his horrible crime. He ran and he ran, tears streaming down his face as the once beautiful garden withered and fell around him, realising that this devastation was the result of his action. Knowing what he had unleashed into the world. He came to a stop by a pool of water which, unlike the surroundings, was calm and tranquil. He sat down on a fallen log, held his head in his hands and wept bitterly."

As Robin spoke, images were forming in Robert's mind. It was as if he was seeing these terrible events unfolding in front of him, as if he were there in that moment. That moment when the world had been changed forever.

"Soon, he became aware of another person beside him. It was the creator. He expected to see hatred and condemnation in her eyes, reproach for the terrible wrong he had committed upon her creation, but instead he saw only tears. Tears of pain like those of his own. When she spoke, it was softly and without aggression.

'You have to see. she told him, 'See what your actions have brought about.'

She waved her hand over the water and, instead of his own reflection, the man saw reflected in it an image of the village his family had built. He saw his house in flames, heard his wife screaming and saw his children and his murdered brother's children fighting each other. On the ground, he realised with a sickening lurch, were the bodies of those who had been killed in the fighting. Not just those of his and his twins' children but those of their other siblings and their children too. The whole family seemed to have turned against one another and the ground was sticky with blood. The look of horror on his face was only matched by those on the faces of his mother and father as he saw them standing in the middle of all the chaos looking with despair as their children and their children's children tore each other apart."

Seeing the scene in his mind's eye, Robert wanted to cry out, to beg Robin to cease telling this story, for the chaos to end but he did not.

"'So it shall now be for all time,' said the creator softly," Robin's voice took on a strange, softly feminine and almost musical tone as he recounted the

Creator's words. "'The fighting may cease for a time but it will begin again. Brother shall see brother as an enemy, as a threat to his own well-being, and no one will trust anyone else. There will be those who lean more towards good and those who lean more towards evil, but the force of evil has now been released in this forest, for it is a garden no longer, and shall feed off the hatred and malice in the hearts of humanity until perhaps one day it will be strong enough to destroy this world completely. See...' She pointed to the image on the water. Above the rioting village a dark cloud had begun to form. The man had thought at first that is was simply smoke from the burning buildings but now he saw that it was more than that. Thicker somehow, darker. 'Already it has begun.'"

"Could nothing be done?" Robert pleaded, looking imploringly at his mentor. "Could the evil not have been stopped?"

"He asked the same thing," Robin replied, "That poor, wretched man who's actions had brought it upon the world, but the Creator told him that, once unleashed, it must be allowed to run its course, to finish what it has started but," Robin looked up, his green eyes flashing with a steely determination, "It could be fought, hindered, resisted. It could not be stopped but it could be slowed, it's impact reduced. The murderer begged to be allowed to take up this task, to fight and defend against this terrible evil that he had released.

'Do you know what you ask?' the creator enquired gently, 'To do such a thing you would have to live for all time, alone, one with the forest. Forever apart from human society.'

'Whatever it takes!' he exclaimed, 'I will do it!'

'If you are sure then,' she said, 'jump into the water. It will change you, make you immortal and you will remain that way until this evil has finally reached its end.'"

"And did he?" Robert asked. Robin narrowed his eyes for a moment, scanning Robert's face. In reply, he went on with his tale.

"Pausing for a moment and staring at the surface of the water which was now clear of images but glowed with a radiant green light, he took a gulp and dived in. As he swam beneath the surface he felt a surge of power pass through his body and at the same time he felt that he was melting away into nothingness. When he reach the far side he surfaced and found that he was no longer a man. He was a spirit, a being of the forest. He felt as one with all around him. He looked around to see the creator but found that she was no longer there. He was alone."

"What became of him?" asked Robert, "Where is he now?"

"He sits before you." Said Robin, before pausing to allow his words to sink in.

"Then you..." Robert began.

"That's right," nodded Robin quietly, "I am responsible for all the darkness and pain you see around you. That I have been permitted to remain to stand against it is both my curse and my gift."

"But I still don't understand," Robert protested, "You have told me where all evil in the world comes from but not what this has to do with my Grandfather of why his best friend turned on him."

"The evil which I unleashed," Robin explained gently, "Is alive. With every evil, selfish, spiteful or thoughtless act it grows stronger. Men speak of the Devil as a fallen angel but it is not so. The Devil, as men call it, this Dark Spirit of evil, is the sum of all the darkness that is in humanity. As the centuries passed it became ever stronger and grew in consciousness and awareness until it became a being in its own right.

I have set myself in opposition to this abomination for more years now than anyone can count.

It was not your grandfather's friend who killed him." Robin placed a hand gently on Robert's shoulder. "When a mortal dies, their body can be occupied by another, if that body remains intact."

"What are you saying?" asked Robert, bitter tears beginning to form at the corners of his eyes.

"The Sheriff, your grandfather's friend, died in his sleep the night before the murder. Once his soul had departed, it was the Dark Spirit who took possession of his body and now rules the people hereabouts with ruthless cruelty."

"Then I must destroy him!" exclaimed Robert. "To avenge the deaths of my grandparents, their household and countless others who have died under his cruel regime!"

"Alas," said Robin, "As I have already told you, he cannot be destroyed, but he can be overcome. You have the power of goodness and love. Such things are poison to him!"

"So what must I do?"

"Fight him. Force him to leave that body. Banish him from this place."

"But if what you say is true," Robert challenged, "Then it will do no good! He will return!"

"True." Robin nodded, "but it may be months, years or even centuries before he does. Do the people not deserve to have their oppression lifted, if only for one hour? Would you begrudge them that?"

"No!" declared Robert, rising to his feet. "I shall stand by your side to fight him and he shall be defeated!"

"I can teach you and I can train you," said Robin, standing by his side, "I can equip you for the battle ahead. But when the time comes, you must face him alone."

Setting his eyes intensely on the horizon, as if staring down the future, Robert clenched both hands into tight fists, steeling his entire being for the task ahead.

When he spoke, it was in measured, determined tones.

"Then so be it!"

The frost lay heavy and white on the forest floor as Holly sat on a fallen log weaving together supple branches from a holly bush with strands of ivy to make a Yule crown. This was to be Robert's first Christmas as a part of their greenwood family and she wanted to celebrate it with style. Soon it would be dark and the guests would begin to arrive.

The clearing was already decorated. A big bonfire had been built in the middle, nice and tall so that the light from its flames would be reflected in the ice on the trees which formed a protective circle around the spacious clearing, making them seem as if they were alive with swarms of fairies, merrily dancing and twinkling in the warm orange glow.

In fact, there were a fair few real fairies in the trees but they had much better things to be doing rather than just sitting around looking pretty!

Holly completed the crown just as the first of those expected arrived. Christmas was the one occasion when all the inhabitants of the forest, mortal and ethereal, would come together and celebrate being alive. Hanging the crown on a branch of a tree and pausing for a moment to adjust the matching one that she wore, Holly went to greet the guests.

There was the charcoal burner and his family, his wife cradling a newborn baby while their other assorted children ran and played around their legs. The woodsmen, farmers, gamekeepers and poachers who all made their living in the forest came together at this time too, their wives and children with them, all celebrating in the warm magical glow of the fire. As well as the human forest dwellers, there were the imps who normally inhabited the caves and tunnels beneath the ground and the many mysterious creatures and beings of the forest, never normally seen by mortal eyes.

More and more guests arrived. Some of the mortals had brought instruments with them and they struck up a tune to which the others began to dance. Soon the human instruments were joined by an altogether more ethereal sound. Holly realised that her father had joined the group and was playing an enchanting harmony on his flute.

She realised that if her father was there, then Robert must be too. She looked up and saw him standing alone on the other side of the fire. She grabbed the crown she had made for him and ran to meet him. He picked her up and twirled her round in the air as she crowned him her Yuletide king.

The dancing and feasting continued in the warm firelight. A figure was moving amongst the revellers, a large, jovial man clad in a red robe with garlands of holly, with its bright red berries, woven into his flowing white hair. As he passed between the folk, they could feel their spirits lifted, invigorated by his presence, and their hearts filled with joy and gladness. Holly blew him a kiss and he blew one back to her.

Holly put her hands on Robert's shoulders and looked upwards. He followed her gaze. Above their heads, hanging from the bow of a tree, he saw a clump of long green leaves with white berries.

"Mistletoe!" she informed him, grinning cheekily.

Robert narrowed his eyes with mock suspicion.

"That wasn't there a moment ago!" he exclaimed. "You've been using those fairy powers of yours again!"

"As if I would do such a thing," Holly replied, trying to look innocent but unable to suppress a giggle. "But anyway, it makes no difference!"

"What do you mean?" asked Robert, genuinely puzzled.

"Well, however it got there, rules are rules!" Holly informed him.

Robert inclined his head towards her and she stretched up on tiptoes.

"Merry Christmas!" she whispered in his ear. Then she kissed him.

Beginnings

"What's the matter?" Robert asked quietly, putting his hand on Holly's shoulder. The party was over and as the remaining guests began to fall asleep around the smouldering embers of the fire, Robert had realised that Holly was not by his side.

It had not taken him long to find her, sat against a tree, still wearing her Yuletide crown. She was sobbing but they did not appear to be tears of pain anger but rather of deep sadness.

"This was always her favourite time of year," Holly looked up, her big brown eyes red and slightly swollen from the tears. Robert sat down beside her.

"Who?" he asked gently. Holly smiled a little and rested her head on his shoulder.

"I never told you about when I was little did I?" she looked up at him as he brushed her golden hair out of her face.

"You've never even told me how old you are," Robert admitted, "I thought perhaps you'd always been as you are now?"

"Well I'm a lot older than you, young man!" she stuck her tongue out at him teasingly, wiping away a few stray tears with the back of her hand, "and I've been this way for a long time but not quite always. I was a baby once, I had a mother," Holly looked sad again for a moment, "she died when I was born. I grew up normally until my fourteenth summer."

"Is that why you were crying?" Robert asked, "Because you're missing your mother?"

"No," Holly said quietly, "I never knew her, although I know my Father misses her terribly. I did meet her once," she looked distant, "Around the time I stopped growing," Robert decided not to question her about this strange statement, accepting that she would explain it when she was ready and that she had someone else on her mind today. "I was thinking about Granny."

"Who's that?" Robert smiled gently, inviting his beloved nymph to share the memories.

"She looked after me when I was little," Holly explained, smiling wistfully, "The forest is a hard place, harsh and dangerous for any vulnerable child, even one like myself, so when my mother died, my father placed me into the care of a close mortal friend of his, a widowed lady who had raised many children and grandchildren and whose husband, a charcoal burner, had been saved by my father from a gang of drunken soldiers who had come across him in the forest and decided to have fun at his expense. No one would ever tell me what my father did to those who had harassed this man but I know that until the day he died no one ever bothered him again, knowing with certainty that he was under the protection of The Hooded Man."

"She sounds like a very special lady," Robert smiled, "She must have been if your father entrusted you to her care."

"She was," Holly smiled, remembering the wonderful old lady, "Very special indeed. She lived in a little cottage in the forest. That's why I was safe there. My father had told her that I must never leave the forest. I found out why some years later but I didn't know at the time. I was just a happy little child.

For the first ten summers of my life Granny looked after me in her little cottage in the forest." Holly continued, her mood brightening as she recounted the happy memories to Robert. "Sometimes her family would come and visit, her children, grandchildren and even a few great grandchildren and I played with them as family, although Granny was the only one to ever know the truth about where I came from. To everyone else I was presented as an orphan foundling that Granny had come across abandoned in the forest. If anyone suspected my true nature, as some must have done, they were quiet and accepting. One thing I knew for sure in those first years of my life was that I was loved. Granny was the most wonderful cook and I loved the food that she cooked – delicious pies, vegetables grown in the garden of her cottage and the most wonderful, warm, freshly baked bread you could ever hope to taste.

She taught me how to gather fruits, berries and roots in the forest, showing me which were good to eat and which would make me feel ill. When the autumn came we would spend whole days making jars of delicious fruit jam which we would enjoy through the long dark nights and cold days of winter. When it was dark, Granny would set a huge roaring fire in the fireplace and settle into her big rocking chair. I'd snuggle up on her lap and she'd tell me wonderful stories of fairies, dragons, heroes, princesses and magic until I had almost fallen asleep then she'd tuck me into my big warm bed with the lovely cosy blankets which she had knitted for me herself and kiss me goodnight."

As she spoke, Robert felt his heart warmed by the tender scene she described. He admitted to himself that he had never thought too much about Holly's childhood or where she came from. He had come to accept her as one of the many wonderful and strange inhabitants of the forest. Hearing this new information about her made him feel closer to her than ever before, as if she were confiding a personal secret to him.

"Sometimes there would be other visitors," she continued, "travelling merchants and story-tellers who Granny had met with and helped in the past. They would come and spend maybe one night or two in our warm little cottage, enjoying Granny's wonderful cooking and telling me new stories. Perhaps some of them will have told their own stories, stories about me and the little make-believe adventures they would dream up for me! I hope so. If I ever see any of them again I'll have to ask!"

Chuckling, Robert wondered how many of the wonderful, colourful tales of golden-haired princesses he had heard as a child had begun their existence as stories to amuse the infant Holly. She grinned up at him, her tears all but gone as she told him of those happy years but then she looked sad again, looking away as she spoke.

"I loved Granny very, very much and my life with her was happier than any other I could imagine. She was mortal though and had lived a very long and full life before I was ever born. One night, she left. I watched her. Perhaps it was a dream or perhaps it was real. It certainly felt real and in the morning she was gone from the cottage."

"Just tell it to me as you remember it," Robert suggested gently, stroking her hair to soothe her troubled spirit, "If you want to, that is. You don't have to if you're not ready."

"No," she smiled softly, "I want to tell you. It was a warm night towards the end of my eleventh summer. Granny had told me some stories and tucked me up in bed as normal but instead of going to her own bed, she had returned to the rocking chair and sat staring into the fire as if thinking very deeply about something. She nearly always had a smile on her face but the smile she wore that night was different from any I had seen before. It was a peaceful smile, calm and serene, almost like it expressed relief, the kind a traveller feels when they come within sight of a welcoming inn at the end of a very long journey. I did not think too much about it at the time and fairly soon drifted off to sleep.

I don't know how long I slept for but it was before dawn when I stirred. I think it was the breeze across my face which awakened me. I sat up and rubbed my eyes, seeing that the door to the cottage was wide open. I got out of bed and went to investigate. I saw Granny standing just outside the cottage, looking out into the forest. She turned and saw me.

'Come back inside, Granny!' I chided her, 'You'll get cold out here.'

'No my darling,' she replied gently, 'Tonight I'm going home.'

'But this is your home!' I exclaimed, 'Here with me!'

What she said next should have made me sad but it didn't. I think it's because I could see the pure joy radiating from her face."

Saying nothing, Robert put his arms around Holly and held her close, feeling the beat of her heart and the warmth of her body against him as she continued, feeling safe in his arms,

"'You're a big girl now,' she told me softly, her smile still serene and peaceful, 'Too big for a little cottage like this! All of the forest is your home now!' she waved a hand across the expanse of trees which seemed to be glowing faintly in the darkness with more than just reflected moonlight. 'All of this for you to play, dance, sing, love and live!'

'What about you?' I asked.

'See? Over there?' she pointed towards the distance. 'That's my husband, coming to meet me. We've been apart for ever such a long time and I've missed him so.' I looked where she pointed."

"What did you see?" Robert asked, "Was it only she who could see what she saw or did you too?"

"I saw," Holly replied quietly, "But I don't know if an ordinary mortal could have done, or if any of it was any more than a dream. As I looked, I saw a figure on horseback coming closer. A handsome young man with golden blonde hair like mine. As he reached the fence around Granny's vegetable garden he jumped down from his horse and opened the gate. I looked at Granny. The years seemed to be melting away from her. The wrinkles and furrows in her face became smooth, her stooped shoulders straightened, her hair became thicker, longer and a beautiful dazzling auburn. She knelt down and gave me one last kiss before going to the gate and embracing the man she had loved for so very many years. He helped her up onto his horse them climbed up behind her, taking the reins in one hand and putting the other around her waist. With a click of his tongue, the horse turned and headed back into the forest. I watched until they were out of sight, the light faded and the forest dark once more.

I do not remember returning to my bed but that was where I found myself when I awoke in the morning as the first rays of dawn burst through the windows. I looked around the cottage that had been my home for as long as I could remember, bade it farewell and walked out into the forest that was to be my home from then on. I left the door open so as to invite anyone in need of a home or some shelter to come inside and partake of the warm fire and the delicious jams which still filled the cupboard."

"Is the cottage still there?" Robert asked, "Did you ever go back?"

"Only once," she replied softly, quietly, "many summers later. I saw children playing in the garden and, wafting from the inside, smelt delicious cooking smells. Silently so as not to alarm whoever was inside, I peered through the window and saw a young woman standing at the stove stirring a pot with one hand whilst in the other arm she held a small baby not three months old. I saw that the cottage was a happy place for them, as it had been for me. I crept away without ever having revealed my presence to them. Some days I think about going back to see who lives there now, or even if it is still standing. But then I remember that delightful scene with the mother and her happy, healthy children and decide that that is the best way to leave Granny's cottage, as a happy memory."

His heart overwhelmed with warmth and love, Robert held her close, stroking her hair and wiping away the warm tears which had dripped down her cheeks as she told the last bit of the story.

"Your Granny sounds wonderful," he smiled, kissing her on the forehead, "And I know she loved you very, very much! I can understand why you miss her, especially at fun times like this, but those wonderful memories will never leave you. No one can take those away." He kissed her again. "Thank you for sharing them with me." Holly looked up at him and smiled, her face brightening. "So now I know all about you!"

"Oh I wouldn't say that!" she grinned cheekily, "You don't know everything about me! I have to keep some surprises up my sleeve don't I?"

"Your sleeve?" Robert raised an eyebrow.

"Well," she giggled, "Figuratively speaking!" She adjusted Robert's Yule crown which had slipped slightly and was sitting lopsidedly on his head. Satisfied that it was now straight, she checked her own. "How do I look?" She asked.

"Like a Queen!" Robert beamed, "The Queen of all the Fairies!"

"Well that's good then!" she grinned as Robert stroked the tips of her pointed ears, "Now, do you suppose there's any of that fruit cake left?"

"So that's where you've been!" exclaimed Ket, running up to Robert. "Should have known really!"

Robert kissed Holly on the cheek and she hopped down off his lap. He got to his feet and adjusted his cloak as Holly jumped up into the tree where she sat swinging her legs, waiting to hear what Ket had to say.

"Robin said to come and get you quickly!" Ket explained, "He says it's time. The convoy are on their way now."

"In that case," replied Robert with a roguish smile, "I would say there's no time to lose! Coming?" he called up to Holly in the tree.

"Nah," she shrugged with indifference. "I've got much better things to do than watch you prance around with a bow and arrow, pretending to be some big hero!" She tried not to smirk but couldn't help herself.

"Oh dear", said Robert, feigning hurt "Well in that case…"

Jumping down from the tree, Holly wrapped her arms around Roberts neck from behind, balancing her weight on a single toe.

"Are you joking?" she laughed, "I wouldn't miss this for anything! Not your first great adventure!" She kissed his earlobe playfully and scampered back up into the tree where she sprang from branch to branch, heading towards the branches of the great oaks which overhung the main road through the forest where she would be able to see everything that transpired.

Robert retrieved his bow from where it rested against the trunk of a tree, swung his quiver of arrows across his back and headed off at a run towards the road, ready to put into action all the training the great woodsman Robin had given him.

As he neared the road, he could hear the entourage of carriages carrying the taxes to Nottingham castle and the coffers of the Sheriff just audible in the distance. He slowed his pace, taking care not to make a sound which could give away his presence.

"Pssst", hissed Holly from above him, "Up here!"

Robert looked up and saw his impish companion stretched out along a branch which hung high above the road, a branch which the carriages with their guard would have to pass directly beneath.

Shouldering his bow, he scrambled deftly up the tree and edged his way along the branch until he sat next to Holly, watching intently as the entourage drew closer. As they neared his hiding place he pulled his voluminous hood up over his face and gripped his bow tightly. Holly saw the knuckles of his hand in which he held his bow whiten with tension. She knew that Robert was incredibly nervous thinking of what he was about to do but she also had every faith that he was capable – he was a good, brave man and had been trained well by her father and the other immortals who inhabited the greenwood.

Robert knew that timing was everything. He waited until the carriages were a few yards away then loosed three arrows in quick succession which thudded into the ground less than an inch from the horses' front hooves, causing them to rear up in panic.

Seizing his moment to take advantage of the coach drivers' confusion and panic, he let another arrow fly, this one burying itself deep in the wood just above the first driver's head. The driver of the second coach reached for the crossbow by his side. A further arrow pinned his hand to the bench on which he sat – painful but not fatal.

Taking careful aim, he fired an arrow above their heads, angled precisely so that the shaft brushed the bottom of a branch which hung across the road, causing the path of the arrow to curve and hit the back of the last carriage as if it had been fired from behind.

Robert leapt down from the tree in which he had hidden himself, stringing another arrow even as he did so. He stood in the road, the tip of his arrow aimed squarely at the heart of the first driver.

"Greetings gentlemen," he declared. "Welcome to my forest!"

"Stand aside!" growled the driver. "We serve his majesty the king and we are on his business. Now move aside or I cut you down where you stand!"

The driver went for his sword but before he knew what had happened, an arrow sliced through his palm and deep into his thigh, splintering the bone, leaving his hand pinned to his side and his face contorted with pain. He knew better than to try to pull the arrow out as Robert had another already aimed at him, this time at his throat.

"Anyone else care to make a fuss?" Robert asked of the other drivers, a genial tone in his voice as if he found the whole thing greatly amusing. Silence.

With the practised skill of an acrobat, Robert threw his bow into the air, leapt up to grab the branch he had sat on waiting for the carriages, swung himself forward and landed on top of the first carriages, catching his bow half a second later.

"Now," he said, glaring at the second driver, his hand still securely pinned to the wooden bench, "Who is it you serve?"

"The king!" exclaimed the man, his voice wavering with fear and pain, "We are loyal servants of his majesty!"

Realising the potential she had to enhance the situation, Holly blended her appearance with the trees and swung from branch to branch. All the soldiers could see was a fleeting shadow and sudden movements in the dense canopy. They utterly believed that they were surrounded by an army of bloodthirsty cut-throats. Holly couldn't help but laugh quietly to herself at the look of terror on the men's faces. These brave soldiers who prided themselves on their courage and fearlessness reduced to quivering wrecks by some flashy archery and a little acrobatics. There was something about the forest which tended to tap into people's primal fears, to bring out the superstitious paranoia in the most rational of men. It was certainly working today!

"Then why is it," questioned Robert, his voice and expression darkening, "that you take money from his people, money they cannot afford, so they are forced to live in squalor, without warm clothes to wear in the winter or enough food to feed their children? Why do you take what little they have so they have no choice but to become outlaws in the forest, hunting the king's own deer simply to survive? How can you be loyal to his majesty when you treat his people as if they were animals?"

The third driver who, until now, had been silent spoke up.

"It's our job!" he pleaded, "We are simply following orders. The Sheriff demands the taxes and we must collect them, otherwise he'd have our heads!"

"Oh? The Sheriff?" Robert raised an eyebrow, "I thought it was the king that you served?"

"We do," the man replied, "but the Sheriff is the king's representative in the shire, it's his orders we must follow or face the consequences."

"Well!" Robert flung his arms out in an expansive gesture of welcome, "If that is the case then I see a simple solution. For you see, this forest is my kingdom and the Sheriff has no power here. Here I am the king and it's my word which must be obeyed."

The first driver lunged with his free hand for his crossbow. The arrow sped towards Robert who leapt up, somersaulting in the air as it sailed harmlessly beneath him, landing with a dull clatter on the road some way off.

Almost before his feet touched the roof of the carriage, Robin had let an arrow fly from his bow. Enough warnings had been given. This arrow found its mark and the man's head slumped forward, his body pegged like some obscene puppet by the arrow through his throat.

"Oh dear," Robert shook his head. "I was really hoping it wasn't going to come to that. Still, I trust that I can expect no further trouble from you two fine gentlemen?"

Both soldiers shook their heads hurriedly. Robert leant over and pulled the arrow from the second driver's hand. He gasped and held his bleeding hand tightly with the other.

"Now if you'd be so kind," said Robert, his courteous voice dripping with sarcasm, "unburden yourselves of your heavy load and I shall see it reaches its rightful owners."

"But", stammered the third soldier, "This gold is taxes collected for the Sheriff! If we fail to deliver it…"

"This money," Robert blazed with anger as he shouted, "belongs to the people! This is the money they need to provide food, clothing and shelter! This is not just their money, this is their lives and the lives of their children! The Sheriff has no more right to it than he does to the air they breathe, although I'm sure he'd try to take that for himself too if he could!"

He narrowed his eyes and looked at each of the men in turn.

"If you fear retribution from your cruel master, you are free to stay and serve me instead. Live the life of an outlaw in this forest where every man is free."

"No." said the second man, quietly. "I have a wife and five children. I must return to them but I see now that this money is not the Sheriff's by right. I'll do as you ask if you do me one service in return."

"And what would that be?" Robert asked, surprised that such a man would be asking a favour from him.

"Take my hand. Cut it off so that I can say I fought and was overpowered. With one hand I will be forced to leave the service of the Sheriff, I will be given some small amount of money to compensate for my loss and I can take my family and start a new life. A life somewhere far away from here.

Please, good master, if you care for my family as much as you do for the peasants of the village, you'll do as I ask."

Lowering his eyes, Robert reflected for a moment. Maiming this fundamentally good man was distasteful to him, yet he realised that this would be the only chance the man had to start afresh.

"I'll do as you ask." He told him, "And you," he snapped, swinging round to face the third soldier, "would do well to keep silence, else when I have severed his hand I may turn my attention to your tongue!" The man nodded his acquiescence.

"Now," said Robert, briskly, "unload the chests and pile them by the side of the road. Try anything funny and it will be the last thing you ever do. When you're done with that, load your comrade's body into the back of one and take it back to the city. He deserves a decent burial at least."

Robert jumped up from the top of the coach and back into the branch of the tree.

He and Holly watched as the two men nervously unloaded the chests full of taxed gold and piled them in a neat stack by the side of the road. Robert kept his bowstring pulled throughout, in case he should need to warn them further of his vigilance, but they did as he had commanded. When they had safely stowed the body of the dead soldier into the back of his carriage and hitched it by rope to the others so all three could be led from the front, the injured men stepped forward and, not knowing exactly where Robert was concealed, spoke into the trees above his head.

"Master!" he called, "I have kept my side of our bargain, now I beg you to honour yours!"

Drawing the long, sharp dagger from its sheath in his belt, Robert jumped down from his vantage point and landed behind the man, startling him.

"Hold out you hand." He said, as kindly as he could.

Steely eyed and steadfast, the man held out his hand which was still bleeding from the arrow wound inflicted only scant minutes before. Robert could not help but admire this man's courage and his determination to safeguard his family. His hand did not shake in the slightest as he held it out to be severed.

Bringing his knife down hard and fast on the exposed wrist, Robert cut the hand cleanly from the arm. The man screwed up his face in pain but did not cry out. Quickly, Robert tore a strip of cloth from the man's travelling cloak which was rolled up on the seat next to where he had sat and wrapped it tightly around the bloody stump.

"Bless you, good master." Said the soldier, nodding sincerely to Robert.

"Now go!" Robert commanded. "And when you are asked what happened, tell the Sheriff that you were bested by the man who will not suffer his injustice, the man who will stand against him and all his kind until their tyranny is at an end!"

"But," asked the third soldier, "If he asks who defeated us, what should we tell him? What is your name?"

Pausing for a moment, Robert had the unshakable feeling that his apprenticeship was about to come to an end. That he was about to take his place in history alongside his teacher and mentor, Holly's father.

"My name," he replied, quietly but defiantly, "is Robin Hood!"

With that, he disappeared back up into the trees and the soldiers drove their carriages out on through the forest as fast as they could, lest their attacker rethink his mercy.

Up in the tree, Holly leant her golden head against Robert's shoulder.

"I knew you could do it!" she enthused. "Those men will go back to the city and tell the rest what happened! The Sheriff will know that his reign is not unchallenged!"

As Robert looked down quietly, John emerged from the trees and gathered up the chests in his huge arms. In the morning, Robert knew that the citizens of the village would wake to find their money returned to them, with more besides, but that was not his concern.

"Do you really think I am up to the task?" he asked. "I am, after all, just a man like any other."

"No you're not!" said Holly, her warm hand on his knee, "today you stopped being a man. You became a legend!"

The time had come.

Robert was ready. He knew in his heart that his training was at an end. The time had come at last to fulfil his destiny and do the task he had spent the last year of his life preparing for. To avenge his family. To regain his birthright and free the people from oppression. To defeat the evil Sheriff.

Her head on his shoulder and her golden hair spilling over his chest, Holly slept peacefully but Robert could not rest. His mind was racing. He knew that he was up to the task, Robin had trained him well, but he also knew that he could not afford to make a mistake. If he allowed the Sheriff to defeat him then all hope would be gone. There would be no other who could rise up to fight in his place. This was his destiny, and his alone.

The full resources of the forest and all who dwelt within were at his disposal, but their effectiveness was limited. Loxley Manor, the home that rightfully belonged to his family, was surrounded by vast grounds and, attempting to pre-empt any greenwood rebellion, the Sheriff had seen to it that every tree and plant was removed, leaving only barren gravel. Many of the forest dwellers would be able to accompany him to the edge of the forest but no further. They may be able to create a distraction but little more. Ket and Hob could be sent ahead to spy but they were no fighters. Holly, he knew, would weaken away from the forest. On the one occasion she had visited a village with some mortal friends, she had sickened and actually died within an hour, spending the autumn and winter in the ground while her body regenerated, her soul far, far, away, until she had risen in the springtime, many years before Robert's birth. Robert knew that she could not be killed by mortal weapons but she could be hurt. Removing her from the forest, even for a few minutes, exposed her to greater risk than he could bear. Any help she could give him would have to be from back in the forest. She had agreed to lead the others in creating enough of a distraction to allow him to get past the guards into the Sheriff's stronghold.

There remained a problem, however. A problem which could prove his undoing if he did not consider it carefully enough. The Sheriff, although he inhabited a mortal body, was no normal man. He had no human soul. He was the accumulation of countless centuries of evil. All the cruelty, malice and hate which the human race had generated throughout its existence was concentrated and personified in the man that Robert would have to face.

Soothingly, Robert stroked Holly's hair as she murmured in her sleep. He knew that he might never be able to return to her. When he said goodbye at the edge of the forest, it could be forever. Bringing down the Sheriff may very well cost him his own life. He looked down at her sleeping form, curled beside him, so vibrant and beautiful, yet small and vulnerable. The thought of leaving her was almost enough to tear his heart in two. He wondered what would become of her if he were never to return. What would she do? He pushed from his mind the thought that she had lived for over half a century before he came into her life. He could not imagine either of them in a world that they did not share.

Kissed her tenderly on the top of her head, Robert carefully eased himself up, leaving her resting against the tree-stump on which he had supported himself. In the winter months, when the frosts were harsh and the nights bitter, he slept underground in the sandstone caves and tunnels which riddled the area, but when the air was warm and the nights short, he preferred to sleep beneath the stars, reminding him how each tiny piece of the cosmos unites to form the whole, each in its place and with its own unique task to fulfil. He stood up and stretched.

Walking some distance to avoid disturbing Holly, Robert gave a high-pitched whistle. There was a slight rustle in the undergrowth and suddenly, apparently from nowhere, Robert was joined by two small, squat figures with wild hair and even wilder faces – Ket and Hob.

"Right boys," he began, "we need to know exactly when the guards are at their most vulnerable. We'll only get one shot at distracting them when the time comes, otherwise they'll get suspicious and we need to know exactly when."

Looking towards the horizon, Robert saw that it was already tinged with a thin line of pink.

"It's nearly dawn now. We'll have to attack in the daylight. I don't know what unearthly creatures or traps the Sheriff has at his disposal and I certainly don't want to be blundering around near the Manor in the dark!"

Ket and Hob shifted uncomfortably, they seemed slightly worried that Robert was planning to spring a surprise attack then and there!

"Today we just watch", Robert continued, putting them at their ease. "We'll stay all day if we have to. The Sheriff has more people, better weapons and more power than us. If we're to have any chance of beating him, we have to be cleverer!"

"Now wait just a minute!"

The voice came from behind them. Robert swung around to see Holly standing there, her hands on her hips and his hooded cloak slung over her arm. Clearly she had not been as deeply asleep as he thought!

"You're not going anywhere without me!"

She laughed playfully and threw his cloak to him. Robert swung it around his shoulders and fastened it at the neck. Holly could render herself invisible to mortal eyes, except those who knew how to look, and Ket and Hob were practised masters at hiding as if they were not there, even in the most exposed of areas, but with his cloak pulled around and the hood covering his head, Robert found that he could disguise himself fairly effectively in the shadowy recesses of the forest. This cover would certainly suffice for today's task.

As nimbly as any squirrel, Holly scurried up into the tree-tops to scout ahead for any danger and the rest of the party set off for the edge of the forest which bordered the Manor's grounds.

As they neared the border, they all noticed a definite change. Whereas in the main body of the forest the trees were covered with lush green leaves, the nearer to the edge they came, the more withered the leaves appeared, giving way eventually to bare trees. The bark of these trees was not the warm brown, orange or silver of elsewhere in the forest, but a sad, lifeless grey. No birds sang in the branches and no small creatures made their homes in the hollows or the scrubby, dry foliage beneath. It was as if nothing could live with the prolonged exposure to such pure, concentrated evil.

With a light crunch of dried leaves and twigs, Holly dropped down from the tree and landed next to Robert. She took his hand, unsure whether she meant the gesture for his comfort or her own. This part of the forest made her feel ill. She felt sinister, invisible forces all around them, as if countless unearthly eyes were watching them from all around, plotting their doom. She thought it highly unlikely that the Sheriff would not know of their presence, she just hoped against hope that when the time came their distraction would be enough to get Robert in. After that, everything would be up to him.

Despite the rising sun, the edge of the forest was dark and shadowy.

The group waited silently, watching the building and the grounds as the hours ticked by. Two large man-like creatures patrolled the outside with monstrous hounds. Robert theorised that the best time to try to gain access would be when they met around the far side. If Holly and her gang would be able to hold their attention at that furthest point, he would be able to cross the expanse between the forest and the building. He was fairly confident that the acrobatic skills which Holly had taught him would enable him to evade any arrows or other missiles which came at him from the windows, but reaching the Manor was the easy part – it was once he was inside that he would be in real danger.

Finally, dusk began to fall. At Robert's signal, they all quietly moved back into the forest. It was a relief to be away from the Manor house and the horrible, all-encompassing feeling of evil which pervaded the grounds. The further away they got, the warmer the air around them became, and the greener the trees. Robert wanted nothing more than to never return to that accursed place again but he knew he must. After sitting down with the others, over some hastily prepared food, to discuss their final strategy for the next day, Robert lay down under the stars and tried to relax himself enough to sleep but it was almost impossible.

Nestling by his side, Holly watched him starring up at the sky, unable to rest. She wound his hair around her fingers and sung to him gently. The ancient, lilting songs which her father had sung to her when she was a baby and needed to be soothed. Gradually his eyelids closed and his breathing became steady.

"Peaceful dreams." Holly whispered before kissing him gently on the cheek and allowing herself to drift off to sleep.

The next morning, Robert awoke alert and refreshed. He gathered the gang together then strapped his sword to his side, slung his full quiver of arrows over his shoulder, seized his bow and set off towards the edge of the forest.

As arranged, Robert stayed alone at the spot where they had watched from the previous day while Holly and the others moved silently through the shadows to the far side of the building. Robert watched the guards cross in front of him then continue their patrols round the walls. He knew that when he had counted to one hundred and twenty, they would cross again at the other side at which point Holly and her team would distract them – that would be his chance to cross the expanse before him.

As he reached the requisite number, he heard a terrible commotion with shouts and screams. He did not have time to worry about Holly or the others. He would just have to trust them to do their job safely and make sure he fulfilled his role properly.

He pulled up his hood and sprung forward. Despite his wariness, no attacks came from the windows. It seemed as if no one had noticed him approaching, although he was not so naïve as to suppose that no dark force watched him from the shadows.

Having reached the wall, he edged his way around the wall of the building which had been his home for so many years, past the heavy oak doors, round to the entrance he hoped the Sheriff did not know about – the entrance through the cellar. Praying that the distraction would last long enough, he found the spot where a tangle of dead grass and weeds obscured the iron trapdoor.

Ripping the dried, matted foliage aside, he heaved the hatch open. The hatch had not been opened in years and the hinges were rusted but Robert was able to lift it enough to slip inside. The hatch did not close behind him and Robert was grateful for the small amount of light it let in.

Slipping his bowstring over his arm, Robert drew his sword and crept towards the stone steps which led up to the pantry in the kitchen. He could hear footsteps in the room above and the muffled sound of voices. Although he could not make out their words, there was no urgency in their tone. It didn't sound like they were on the lookout for an invader, rather that they were just making conversation and going about their business.

Trying to keep his breath shallow and quiet, Robert waited until a few minutes later he heard the footsteps move to one end of the room and the sound of a door closing. After waiting a few moments more to make sure that everyone had gone, Robert made his way up to the top of the steps and through the door above.

He knew that there were hidden passages within the walls which led between the rooms undercover. As a boy he had often used a passage behind a secretly hinged panel hidden by a tapestry on his bedroom wall to sneak down to the kitchen and help himself to food from the kitchen without the cook noticing. He realised with a pang of sadness that the cook, who had always been more like an aunt to him, had most likely been murdered along with all the other servants and that possibly her body roamed the building even now, unable to rest and animated by some unholy force.

Out of necessity, he pushed the thought from his mind. There would be time to mourn later, when this was all over. Now was the time for action!

Making his way carefully across the kitchen, illuminated only by the shaft of dust-filled light which broke in through the single narrow window high up on the wall, Robert felt for the concealed doorway in the apparently solid wooden pillar. The door gap was narrower than he remembered, but he breathed in and slid through sideways. Beyond the doorway, the passageway was a little wider and Robert was able to relax a little. The cobwebs, which he brushed aside with his outstretched sword, left him reasonably confident that the passage had remained undiscovered since he left.

His confidence did not last long. Standing in the small corridor before the narrow spiral staircase, Robert heard a strange scratching sound above his head. There was a faint plop as a glob of foul-smelling liquid landed on the dusty floor beside Robert's boot. His heart racing with apprehension, Robert looked up to the ceiling of the chamber.

Above his head, clinging to a vast, sticky web, sat an enormous spider. Each of its eight spindly legs easily the length of a grown man's arm. It scuttled forward, dislodging something from the web. The object hit the floor with a dry clatter. It was a bone, the flesh stripped from it and the marrow sucked from within. A human bone.

Tucking its legs up by its side, the spider descended on a silken thread until it hung in front of Robert, its multiple, inhuman eyes level with his face. It hissed at Robert, as if it was not quite sure how to react to this intruder in its den.

Desperately, Robert groped for the doorway he had made his way through moments before but it could not be found. Hidden by some dark enchantment. The spider studied Robert for a moment more, then dropped to the floor and scurried backwards into the darkness. Robert now had no idea where the beast had gone.

Tentatively, sword in hand, Robert took a step forward, only to leap back an instant later, his heightened instincts having warned him of a spray of corrosive venom which the beast had spat in his direction.

A second spurt hit the wall near his head, causing the stone to fizz and dissolve. Robert stepped boldly out into the middle of the chamber. The spider sprang at him but he plunged his sword deep into the monster's repulsive body, piercing the venom sack.

A demonic shriek issued from the spider as its insides were eaten away by its own poison. Disgusted, Robert threw down his sword, the blade of which was now useless, corroded beyond repair, beside the writhing beast. He stood and watched for a short while longer until the thing stopped moving and he could be sure that it was dead.

Trying desperately not to notice the desiccated human remains which lay scattered upon many of the steps, Robert ascended the spiral stairs up to what had been his bedroom, reaching the top without further obstacle or attack.

At the top, Robert released the catch behind the secret panel and slid it aside. The tapestry which normally concealed this doorway was gone and he suddenly felt horribly exposed as he stood there, blinking rapidly to allow his eyes to adjust to the bright daylight which streamed in through the window.

As he looked around, he saw a small figure asleep in the bed which had once been his. The figure was moving ever so slightly under the covers and Robert could hear a faint sob. Who was this person? A child held captive by the Sheriff? He crept forward gently so as not to alarm the occupant of the bed. Long red hair concealed the persons face, but it appeared to be a small girl. Robert stretched out his hand and touched her on the shoulder.

"Don't be afraid," he whispered soothingly, "I'll get you out of here."

The figure sat bolt upright in the bed. Not a human child at all but some hideous imp or half-ling.

"Turn back Robin Hood!" it snarled. "Turn back or be damned!"

Shocked, Robert stumbled back and went for his bow but the creature burst into flames before his eyes, laughing with a maniacal frenzy. The flames lasted only for a moment, subsiding to leave no evidence of the creature's presence, except for a small scorched patch on the sheets. Robert touched the burned fabric. It was cold.

Undeterred, Robert pressed forward and burst through the door, grabbing hold of the handle for dear life as he realised that the landing was gone.

Carefully, Robert pulled himself back up into the doorway, sat on the polished wooden floor and surveyed the scene below.

The grand reception lobby of the manor had been gutted. The statues smashed, landings and staircases ripped apart and the walls scorched black by diabolical flames. All that remained of the previous decoration were the torches resting in holders on the wall, all burning and casting sinister shadows amongst the rubble.

Alarmed, Robert stood up as he saw another door, directly opposite where he sat, swing open.

There, silhouetted by the sunlight which was coloured a suitably demonic red hew by the stained glass of the window behind him, stood the Sheriff. Or rather, Robert thought to himself, the thing which had taken possession of the Sheriff's body.

Taking aim, Robert immediately let fly an arrow which the Sheriff caught inches from his chest. The wooden shaft burst into flames and the Sheriff brushed the ash from his hand before speaking in a calculating, derisive voice.

"Oh come now," he sneered, "Is that really the best you can manage? I'm afraid you'll have to try much harder than that!"

"Then come here!" cried Robert, across the expanse, "And face me like a man!"

"Now why would I want to do that?" asked the Sheriff, his voice dripping with languid sarcasm. "I'm not a man. Why should I face you like one?"

"No. You're no man." Robert concurred. "A coward is what you are! A filthy murdering coward!"

His face flaring with anger, the Sheriff vanished from his archway. An instant later, Robert realised that the demon now stood behind him.

"A coward am I?" he roared. "Let's just see how brave you really are, oh great hero Robin Hood! Or," he spoke softly, dangerously, "Young Earl of Loxley!"

Quicker than a human eye could perceive, he grabbed Robert round the throat with one hand and held him out over the gulf. Robert struggled with all his strength against the Sheriff's hold, preferring to fall to his death than be in this abomination's power, but the grip was like iron and he could not pry away the fingers. He spat in his adversary's face.

"Then you know me?" He asked.

"My dear boy. The wonderful thing about taking control of another's body is that I know everything that he knew. I remember you as a small boy, as a whiny adolescent, and now here you are. All grown up. But," he continued, in a voice which was both elegant and deadly, "Do you suppose for one moment I'd have mistaken a mortal, a mere child like yourself, for the real Robin Hood, as he now calls himself?"He snorted derisively. "Do you really think?" he hissed, "that I could mistake a snivelling brat like you for my own father!"

He pulled Robert back inside and flung him to the floor. Robert massaged his bruised throat as the Sheriff turned away.

"Robin is not your father!" he retorted. "He told me all about you. I know what you are!"

"Then," cried the Sheriff, spinning round to face him once more, "You also know why I am!"

The Sheriff advanced on Robert, who got shakily to his feet. The Sheriff stopped face to face with Robert, their eyes level and their noses almost touching.

"You know," he hissed, "That it was his evil which gave me life! His callous cruelty which brought me forth and has allowed me to feed on human greed and wickedness ever since."

"Robin has vowed to destroy you!" Retorted Robert. "He has condemned himself to walk the earth for an eternity, until you are utterly destroyed!"

"Why do you suppose," snarled the Sheriff, "that he sent you here to fight me? It's because he dare not look upon me. Dare not face the truth."

"What would you know about truth?" Robert grimaced.

"The truth," the Sheriff's breath felt cold against Robert's face, "The truth is that he is responsible for my existence. All evil in the world is his responsibility. All blood spilled," he declared triumphantly, "is on his hands!"

"Then that is why he sent me!" Robert pushed the demon aside with a swipe of his hand, so that he now stood with his back to the window. Away from the odious presence of the bestial thing which wore a human face.

"Robin may have brought forth evil. But now he brings forth good! And it is with the power of good that I shall fight you and, make no mistake, I shall destroy you."

"Good?" mocked the Sheriff. "I can see the darkness in your heart. The evil which riddles your soul like a cancer. I see your depraved desires. Your filthy lusts. But most of all, I see your desire for vengeance."

Robert's face hardened as the Sheriff continued to taunt him.

"You hate me. You hate me with your entire being. That hate drives you to vengeance and unleashes the evil which you try oh so very hard to keep locked up in that frail human heart of yours. Your hate feeds me. Makes me stronger. And that is why you shall die by my hand today!"

In an instant, Robert knew what he must do. He knew what Robin had known all along. Why he had to come here alone and why it was only he who could defeat the Sheriff.

"Then I shall not fight." He said quietly.

"You accept your fate? Then prepare to die!"

The Sheriff swooped forward but Robert held out his hand.

"No." He said, without raising his voice. "I forgive you."

"What?" the Sheriff growled.

"I forgive you." Robert repeated simply.

The Sheriff staggered and his knees gave way as Robert continued to speak.

"I see now that you do only what it is in your nature to do. I have no hatred in my heart for you. I forgive you. Go free with my blessing."

An unholy red aura began to surround the Sheriff as the demon within him struggled to maintain control of the human body. Finally, with an unearthly scream, a plume of iridescent fire shot upwards from the Sheriff's mouth and the body slumped to the floor. Empty.

Robert wanted nothing left. Nothing to remind him of the hatred he had felt, of his thirst for vengeance against his family's murderer. Remembering what Robin had told him, about the Dark Spirit being only able to possess a body which remained intact, Robert carried the body of his grandfather's friend back down the passageway.

No fear left within him now, Robert pushed open the door of the kitchen which led into the ruined hall. He laid the body on a heap of charred wood in the centre and, taking a torch from the wall, ignited the pyre.

Throwing the torch down, he turned his back and walked slowly out of the grand entrance, the doors of which swung open as if to admit him back out into the glorious sunlight.

As he walked across the grounds, he turned and looked back at the building which had once been his home.

The black smoke rising above formed for a moment into the semblance of a human face.

"This is not the end Loxley!" it cried. "As long as there is evil in the world, I shall never be vanquished!"

But Robert did not care. He turned his back on the evil face and the burning remains of Loxley Manor, defiled and spoilt forever, and walked back to the forest. His new home.

Taking careful aim, Robert pulled back his bowstring and let the arrow fly, hitting its target dead centre. Holly clapped and he gave a theatrical bow, grinning at her up in the tree. She loved to watch him practice, particularly on a day like this when the summer breeze caused his long brown hair to waft gently like the leaves in the trees that rustled around her as she watched.

Springing down from the branch with practised ease, she went to inspect the target.

"Hmm, bit wonky this time," she said, pulling the arrow from the matted straw. "Not up to your usual standard!" She shook her head in mock-reproach.

"It's all your fault!" He teased. "You moved the target with those fairy powers of yours, it's a wonder I could hit the thing at all!"

Her hands on her hips, Holly opened her eyes and mouth wide in mock outrage.

"Such scurrilous accusations!" she cried. "I would never do such a thing!"

"Sure." replied Robert, "Whatever you say!"

Unable to maintain her act and longer and breaking into a giggle, Holly looked up into his laughing face with his twinkling brown eyes, pointed beard and playfully tangled hair – so like her father in many ways and yet not.

Plucking another arrow from the quiver slung across his back, Robert aimed at the target.

"None of your games this time!" He told Holly, winking cheekily.

Pulling back the bowstring, Robert readied himself to release another arrow. Holly stood behind him and gently, ever so subtly, nudged the lower tip of his longbow with her big toe, causing the arrow to fly off at a wild angle and its tip in the trunk of a tree several yards to the right of the target.

"Dear oh dear", she sighed, biting her lip to avoid laughing out loud. "You really don't seem to be on form today!"

"That does it!" Robert shouted, attempting to look furious but unable to suppress the twinkle in his eye or stop the corner of his mouth twitching. He threw his bow down on the ground. "Come here, you!"

He flung himself towards Holly and she neatly sidestepped, causing him to fall flat on the floor, his face full of leaves and mud. Robert jumped up again and started to chase Holly who ran laughing from tree to tree, almost letting him get close enough to catch her, but never quite, finally jumping up into the lower branches of one of the many wide spreading oak trees.

Close on her tail, Robert scrambled up behind her but, mortal as he was, he was unable to match her elfin agility. Just as he managed to clamber on the branch where she sat, she sprang down onto the forest floor, looking up at him and sticking out her tongue. Suddenly the branch, straining under the weight of a grown man, gave way and Robert found himself once more sprawled on the ground. Holly went to run again but Robert stretched out and grabbed her ankle so she too fell to the ground, giggling.

Seizing his opportunity, Robert pounced on her and tickled her until she shrieked with laughter. She retaliated and soon the two of them were soon rolling around together in the leaves, laughing uncontrollably. When neither could take any more, they sat up trying to get their breath back. Robert put his arm round Holly's shoulders and she rested her head on his chest.

"So what happens now?" asked Holly.

"What do you mean?" said Robert. "I'll probably get in another hour or so practice then we'll go back to the camp…"

"No." snapped Holly. "I mean, what are you going to do? You've defeated the Sheriff but you can't go back home, you've been declared an outlaw and only the King can pardon you. Anyway," she blushed a little, "we'd all miss you."

"Don't worry," he ruffled her hair playfully, "You don't get rid of me that easily!" He kissed her forehead, "I'm not going anywhere just yet."

His smile vanished and his face darkened. Holly thought that she could see just a little of the fire that burned in her father's eyes when he was seized by great anger or passion.

"The Sheriff may be gone, for now," he said grimly, "but he will return, stronger and more evil than ever. In the mean time, there is still much darkness in the world. Hate, injustice and cruelty. The world still needs Robin Hood and, as long as they do, I shall be here."

"Anyway," he said as he stood and brushed the leaves off his clothes, suddenly much brighter, "Enough talk! I don't know about you but I'm starving!"

Seizing his bow, Robert let fly an arrow into the branches of the trees above his target. There was a slightly wet, crunching sound then the arrow dropped. Holly sprang over to catch it before it hit the ground. Neatly impaled along its shaft were two golden apples, the juice trickling along the arrow and dripping stickily from the point.

She pulled one off and handed it to Robert then started to munch her own still stuck on the arrow. Robert leant up against the tree where his target was hanging, looking at it thoughtfully. Holly jumped suddenly as Ket spoke, seemingly appearing out of nowhere.

Although Ket could not conceal himself from mortal eyes the way Holly and her father Robin could, he had an amazing ability to sneak around unseen. Robert found it slightly unnerving at times. He had learned over the time he had known them to sense Robin and Holly's presence even when he could not see them – the tell-tale rustles in the tree which sounded just like the breeze to an untrained ear, or the way all the plants and trees seemed just that little bit more alive and vibrant when they were nearby; again, unnoticeable to an ordinary visitor to the forest but unmistakeable for a person who knew what they were looking for. Ket and his brother, on the other hand, could still catch him off guard and Robert was a little uneasy about the fact that he never knew when one of them might be watching him!

"I've brought news!" cried Ket, his voice surprisingly loud coming from him. Not exactly human, though certainly a physical, mortal being, Ket was very short and squat, the nails of his fingers rather claw-like and his mouth too large for his face.

"I do wish you wouldn't keep doing that!" snapped Holly, throwing her apple core at him but without malice. Ket grinned a very wide, toothy smile.

"A fellow has to have some fun!"

Narrowing her eyes, Holly gave him her best attempt at a withering look and stuck out her tongue. Robert knew how she felt but was also curious to hear the news Ket was bringing. He finished his apple and dropped the core by his feet, wiping his sticky hand on his tunic.

"So?" He asked, "You're not going to make us guess are you? What's your news?"

"The people wish to honour their great hero!" He declared, with a grand sweep of his arm, "They wish to pledge their thanks to bold Robin Hood!"

"But I am an outlaw!" exclaimed Robert. "If I show my face publicly I'll be arrested immediately, imprisoned and probably executed!"

"Only to the authorities," explained Ket with a sly grin. "To the people you are a hero! They have a gift of thanks for you but they know that you can't make yourself known, so they have devised a cunning scheme to honour you in a public celebration, whilst preserving your anonymity!"

"But how...?" Asked Robert, struggling to see how such a thing could be done.

His grin widened to almost unimaginable proportions, Ket was clearly enjoying imparting this news and was trying to string it out as long as possible. Holly fought back a very strong urge to throw something else at him and warn him what she would do with the arrow which she still held if he didn't get on with it. Instead she shot him a slightly murderous glance which caused him to forget his train of thought for a second or two. Fearing for his life and personal safety, he quickly regained his composure.

"Everyone knows that you are the greatest archer in the land!" Ket wheedled, "So they know that any archery contest you enter you're sure to win by a clear margin."

"Therefore...?" Holly rolled her hand telling him to get to the point.

"Therefore, they have devised this tournament with a silver arrow for the winner which they know is sure to be you! It's much safer than just calling you out in public."

"A silver arrow?" Robert gasped.

"Solid silver!" confirmed Ket, proudly, "made by the finest silversmith in the kingdom. Well," he smiled slyly, "the finest human silversmith anyway."

Taking a moment to reflect, Robert felt overwhelmed by what Ket was telling him. It was not so much the value of the arrow that excited him. After all, he had stolen fifty times it's worth from the corrupt merchants and in "reclaimed" taxes in the last six months alone but he was delighted by the thought that the people he worked so hard to help, whose suffering he sought to alleviate, would appreciate him enough to honour him in such a fashion.

"When is the tournament?" he asked.

shuffling his feet and avoiding their eyes, Ket looked rather embarrassed. Holly wondered what could produce such a reaction in the normally over-confidant fellow.

"Well?" asked Holly, "When is it?"

Under his breath, Ket mumbled something with neither Holly nor Robert could catch.

"Oh come on, speak up!" snapped Holly, exasperated, "You seem to know everything about this tournament! So when is it?"

"Well that's just the thing," murmured Ket, sheepishly, "I forgot to ask!"

As it turned out, they did not have to wait very long to find out the date of the tournament.

The tournament was big news with everyone who passed through the forest. Some people were excited about meeting the great Robin Hood in person and others were simply looking forward to the first great social gathering since the oppressive regime of the Sheriff had been overturned by Robert and his gang. Already stories had started circulating, becoming wilder and more dramatic with each retelling. Holly was amused that in a less than a year, Robert had managed to inspire almost as many legends as her father!

Despite her amusement, however, Holly could not help feeling a sense of unease. There was something about the situation which just didn't feel right. Although everyone seemed happy and excited about the contest, she felt a sinister undercurrent in the air, like a dark shadow hanging over the preparations.

The day of the contest arrived. Holly could not shake her feeling of unease and begged Robert not to go, but he said that he could not let the people down. They had prepared this event to celebrate the freedom he had given them and to thank him so he felt it was his duty to attend.

The contest was to be held in the village so Holly knew that she would not be able to attend herself but she was determined that Robert should not go alone so she called Ket and Hob to meet her in secret.

While both forest-dwelling brothers were relatively human in appearance, they were far shorter, no taller than an average five year old child. It meant that although they could travel around the forest and villages unnoticed when they wanted to, to gather information or simply to spy on the mortals for fun, it would not help them to blend in. With one sitting on the other's shoulders, however, with a long cloak to cover them, they would make one passable, if not particularly attractive, human.

After some argument about who should go on top, Ket arguing that he had the less alarming face but Hob arguing that he was significantly lighter and therefore easier to carry, they arranged themselves into the required formation. Holly had to turn her back to giggle while they were arguing as they were twins and, to her eyes at least, completely identical!

She instructed them to stay close to Robert but not to let him notice them if they could help it and not to interfere unless it appeared that he was in danger.

"Do be careful, Promise me!" Holly stood on tip-toes to kiss Robert, her arms around his neck. "I wish that I could come too, to watch you, but I cannot leave the forest."

"I promise," Robert smiled down at her, stroking her hair. "And I know you would be there if you could. I'll make sure I tell you absolutely everything about it when I get back!

After sharing another kiss and assuring Holly that he would maintain constant vigilance, Robert set off towards the village, his trademark hooded cloak around his shoulders and his trusty bow in his hand.

The contest had more of the air of a carnival, with games of skill and chance presided over by jovial travelling showmen, minstrels performing ballads of the amazing adventures of the heroic Robin Hood and market stalls selling all manner of goods including clothing and carved wooden toys. Particularly popular seemed to be child-sized hooded cloaks made from sack-cloth , coloured a garish green with cheap vegetable dye and miniature bows with blunt-ended arrows so the children could emulate their hero.

Chuckling to himself, Robert realised that not drawing too much attention to himself would not be as difficult as he had anticipated. Looking around he could see that many men seemed to have adopted the hooded cloak, in various shades of green, perhaps in the hope that they could convince the locals that they were the guest of honour and possibly even win the silver arrow for themselves.

Feeling a frantic tugging on his cloak, Robert heard a small but excited voice:

"Pappa! Pappa!"

Turning, he saw a small boy who had clearly mistaken him for his father who was, Robert mused, no doubt one of the countless other men in similar attire. The boy realised his mistake at one and grinned sheepishly.

"Sorry Mister!" he chirped happily, "Have you heard? Robin Hood's coming today! Robin Hood!"

Kneeling down, Robert ruffled the boy's hair and grinned, knowing that he had the chance to make the boy's day.

"He's already here!" he winked at the boy who gaped in open-mouthed wonder. Robert put his finger to his lips to warn the boy not to tell anyone then disappeared into the crowd, leaving the boy in star-struck silence with a grin which threatened to split his head in two.

From the steps of the large stone cross in the centre of the village green, a lone official in elaborate robes of office blew his trumpet to gain everyone's attention. Having done so, he announced in a voice which carried across the whole festival:

"The contest for the silver arrow will now begin! Will all those wishing to compete please make their way immediately to the arena!"

The moment had come. Robert made his way through the bustling throng to the roped off area where a large straw target had been set up. He took his place beside the seven other men who had lined up to try their luck behind a line of chalk on the grass one hundred paces before the target. He was amused to note that three of them wore green cloaks. Besides them, there was a dark-skinned man in an elegantly embroidered tunic with an elaborately carved bow of a deep red wood which Robert did not recognise, there were two peasants who seemed like they were just joining in for fun and an arrogant-looking man in a soldier's uniform. The other contestants were conversing amiably and wishing each other luck but the last man stood alone and aloof, clearly believing that the contest was already won. He had not reckoned on the competition.

"The rules are simple!" announced the official. "One arrow each. The closest to the centre of the target shall be deemed the winner and receive the silver arrow!"

The older of the two peasants went first. There were calls of encouragement from his family and a good-natured applause from the crowd when his arrow struck the outer rim of the target. Second went the dark-skinned man. With a look of total concentration, he let fly an arrow which buried itself into the central ring of the target, just to the left of dead-centre. The crowd cheered and he bowed graciously.

Next came one of the hooded men. A hushed air of anticipation hung over the watching crowd as he took aim but his arrow came no closer to the centre than the third ring in! The disappointment was clear – this was obviously not Robin Hood.

Encouraged by cheers and whistles from his supporters in the crowd, the younger peasant took his turn, faring slightly better than his friend but not by much, then the second hooded man took his turn and the arrow struck just on the edge of the inner circle. Close, but not close enough to mark him as the winner.

Sneering at the crowds' jeers and boos, the soldier stepped forward. Silence was called for and he took aim but just before he fired, a hunched, ugly figure in a long cloak which completely covered their body coughed loudly. The soldier lost his concentration at the last second and his arrow flew over the target a good two feet above even the outer rim. He was so furious he snapped his bow across his knee, threw it down in disgust and stormed off, followed by the derisive laughter of the crowd.

Now there were only two contestants left. Robert and the other hooded man. The man stepped forward and once again an expectant hush fell over the audience. His arrow flew straight and true, hitting the dead centre of the target! The crowd roared with admiration, convinced that this man was their hero and saviour. The man lowered his hood and took a sweeping bow.

So like Robert did this man look that they could easily have been taken for brothers, if not mistaken for each other by someone who did not know either of them very well. Many villagers pointed and confirmed to anyone within earshot that this was indeed Robin Hood.

The crowd were elated but from his vantage point on Hob's shoulders, Ket could see that this man's eyes had no human light in them. Though his face was smiling he had the cold, dead eyes of the Dark Spirit. The spirit who had until recently inhabited the body of the Sheriff.

"Wait!" cried Ket, as the crowd seemed ready to declare this man the winner on the spot, "There's one more contestant!"

"What's the point?" called one voice, "We already have a winner!"

"Let him shoot!" retorted another, "What's the harm eh?"

The man's smile, Ket observed, faltered for a moment as the official once again called for silence, although it was probably too quick for most of the watchers to have noticed.

"Will the final contestant please take his shot?" cried the official and the Dark Spirit, who Robert had not yet recognised, stepped back to allow Robert his chance, confident that he would not be able to beat his shot.

Thinking of Holly, and knowing how important it was to the people of the village that he win, Robert pulled back his bowstring and let his arrow fly. It rocketed through the air at amazing speed and split his competitor's arrow in half, straight down the middle, burying itself so deep in the target that its tip protruded from through the other side. There could be no doubt that this was the winning shot. The crowd surged forward, pulling aside the ropes which had marked the boundary of the arena, to lift Robert up onto their shoulders. Ket hurriedly jumped down from Hob's shoulders. It was imperative that they not lose sight of the Dark Spirit. He would not have made an appearance today if he did not have some form of vengeance in mind. He had disappeared into the crowd but they split up, determined to find him before he could cause any harm to Robert.

The people set Robert down at the foot of the cross and he knelt while the official mounted the steps.

"To you, the winner of today's tournament, an much more besides" intoned the official, remembering the necessity not to admit to knowing Robert's true identity, "We present this silver arrow in recognition of your skill with the longbow, and with our thanks."

He was handed a velvet cushion on which rested an exquisite arrow, fashioned from pure silver. Robert stood and received it with a gracious bow, then turned to the crowd and held it aloft. The crowd roared their approval once more, but as they did so, a swirling, dark cloud began to form behind him, slowly but surely taking on human form.

"Run!" yelled Ket and Hob from their places in the crowd, "Run for your lives!"

Spinning around to face the threat, Robert backed away, dropping the arrow on the ground, as the crowd scattered in terror. The dark cloud had now become a man. The man who had so nearly beaten him in the contest.

"So we meet once more, Loxley." He sneered. "Or is it Robin Hood? Names are such transient things after all. I myself have had several. But it makes no matter now."

Ket and Hob ran to Robert's side but he gestured for them to stay away. "Run to the forest." He called. "I can deal with him myself!"

"But..." Hob stammered, "Holly said..."

"I'm quite capable of imagining what Holly said!" Robert snapped, "Go to her now! And if I don't return tell her..." he paused for a moment, "Tell her I love her."

The two brothers fled in the direction of the forest as he had commanded, but stayed just within its boundaries, so they would be able to report what had happened.

"Love!" the Dark Spirit exclaimed with a horrible leer. "Love? What good is love when you're dead and cold!"

Drawing his sword, he lunged forward. Robert leapt out of his way, pulled his cloak from around his shoulders and flicked it outwards so it wrapped around the man, pinning his arms to his sides long enough to make him drop his sword.

Allowing the cloak to slacken, Robert stepped forward and put his foot on the blade of the sword, preventing his opponent from picking it up. The Dark Spirit became cloud once more, re-forming behind Robert, placing himself between Robert and the stone cross.

"I ask once more," he sneered, "What good is love? What use is love to a man who is cold and without shelter or clothing? What use is love to a woman whose child has died from fever? What use is love to a family whose crops have failed, condemning them to a slow starvation? What?" He asked triumphantly "is the use of love to anyone?"

"What use then," asked Robert, "is that cross behind you? Why do the people erect them in the centre of every village square and green? Why do they need to be constantly reminded of that symbol of love?"

The Dark Spirit's eyes narrowed.

"Because," Robert continued, "with love comes hope and with hope there is always another chance, a reason to carry on, a drive to fight and win against the odds!"

"Pretty words," retorted the Dark Spirit, "But pointless. As no one will ever hear them! You thought you'd killed me before, but you see now you were wrong! Defeat me today and I shall return. But if I kill you, then for all your fine words, all your talk of love and hope, you will be gone forever!"

He clicked his fingers and the sword which had been beneath Robert's foot was back in his hand. He took a swing at Robert's neck but Robert ducked, grabbing the silver arrow which still lay on the grass where he had dropped it, just in front of where he stood.

Standing back up, with his free hand Robert grabbed the wrist of the hand which held the sword, forcing it aside. He pushed the point of the silver arrow to the man's chest, pushing so that he stumbled backwards up the steps of the cross.

"You could never win," said Robert, solemnly, "even if you were to slay me, there would be others to take my place. As long as there is one soul left in the world who can feel love, then goodness will triumph."

"What makes you so sure?" snarled the Dark Spirit with his back against the cross, boldly disregarding the spike against his breast.

"Why am I sure?" repeated Robert, letting go of the man's wrist and placing the palm of his hand against the end of the arrow, "Because I have hope, which is something you can never have."

With that, he rammed the arrow through the man's chest with all the strength so that it pierced his heart and pinned him to the stone cross behind. He stood back and watched as a dazzling white light, which seemed to come from inside the cross itself, surrounded the Dark Spirit.

The man clasped the shaft of the arrow and tried to pull it out, but already his form was becoming less distinct, the darkness of his being pushed aside by the light of hope and love flowing through the arrow's pure silver. He looked up and met Robert's gaze with his cold, evil eyes.

"This is not over!" He growled, as he vanished in the brilliant glow from which Robert had to shield his eyes.

The glare subsided and Robert stepped forward, pulling the arrow from the cross. It was warm and felt somehow radiant, as if it had absorbed the light which had dispelled the Dark Spirit.

The villagers, and others who had fled, slowly began to return to see what had happened. A small crowd, including the official who had presented the arrow, were soon gathered around the steps of the cross.

"You saved us again!" they cried, "God bless Robin Hood!"

Breathing deeply to calm his heart-rate, Robert picked up his cloak and swung it back around his shoulders.

"Take this." He handed the silver arrow back to the official, "And bury it beneath this cross. It should help to protect you from him and his kind. Now I am tired," he told them, "I must go."

The crowd separated, providing a path to let him through so he could return to the forest. As he passed, men clapped him on the shoulder, women blew him kisses and children smiled up at him with joyous admiration.

The people took the arrow and did as Robert had instructed. They buried it beneath the cross where, it is said, it remains to this day.

When Robert reached the edge of the forest. He found Ket and Hob waiting for him.

"Well done, Master Robert!" cried Hob.

"We knew you could do it!" Ket joined in.

"That message you gave us for Holly," asked Hob, cautiously, "do you still want us to tell her?"

"No," said Robert, thoughtfully, "I'll tell her myself. When the time is right."

Into the Darkness

Tightening his cloak against the cold, Robert waited under the tree. The desperate woman had begged him to meet her, claiming that what she had to tell him could not be discussed where others may overhear, claiming she feared for her life if they were to be observed.

So urgent was her plea that Robert had not had time to find Holly or Robin, he had simply come to the meeting point she had specified and was now waiting, the bitter wind biting at his face and fingers.

"Oh the Lord be praised, Master Robin!" The shrill, almost hysterical cry came as Robert looked up to see the woman making her way nervously towards him. "I was so worried you wouldn't be here! I have to talk to you! You have to help!"

"It's okay, my dear lady," Robert smiled, trying to reassure the woman who looked to be nearing her fortieth summer, "I am pledged to help whenever and wherever I can. Please tell me what is troubling you."

"It's not just me!" she told him, her eyes wide, "It's happening through all the villages hereabouts but nobody will speak of it for fear they will fall victim too!"

"What is happening?" Robert gently tried to coax from the terrified woman the cause of her fear.

"The disappearings!" she looked around anxiously as if fearful of being watched, "Young men like yourself, women too, even some little'n's. All just gone!"

"Gone?" Robert asked, "Gone where? Run away?"

"We thought so at first," the woman explained, "You know how the young folk are, thirsty for adventure! But so many..." she looked sad, "Always the best, the finest and prettiest or the strongest. Our communities are collapsing around us and nobody will say a thing for fear that if they do, they will be next! And now..."

"And now what?" Robert asked, taking the woman's hand and enclosing it in both of his to try and calm her enough to tell him what she knew.

"My boy!" she wailed, "My lad, gone! Oh please Master Robin! He's no older than yourself. Just a boy! Bring him back to me!"

"I will do what I can. I promise you." Robert looked into her eyes reassuringly. "Is there anything you can tell me? Anything at all that may help me."

"Only that distant look he got in his eyes."

"Distant look?"

"A few days before he disappeared," the woman explained, "he seemed like his mind was elsewhere. He couldn't settle to anything and sometimes didn't even seem to hear when people were talking to him."

"Perhaps he was planning something?" Robert asked, "A trip or adventure. Did he not say anything to anyone? Have you asked his friends?"

"No one will talk about it," she almost sobbed. "People say that he is gone and I should just accept it but I cannot. Please Master Robin! Find my boy and bring him home!"

Suddenly, there was a noise a few yards away, as if someone were approaching. Looking alarmed, the woman turned and ran with no further word to Robert. Looking up, Robert scanned the   woods around him for the intruder.

A few yards away, a small figure flitted between the trees. Darkness was falling rapidly. If the figure was a small child out alone then it was not safe for them to be out alone. Robert decided to investigate. He would escort the child safely home then go and ask Robin and Holly what, if anything, they knew about these disappearances.

Quickly, so as not to lose track of the traveller, Robert made his way through the trees to where he has seen them. Finding himself standing on a red stone path, he looked in the direction the figure had been travelling. A few yards ahead of him he saw a small girl with dark brown hair. He called to her but she did not respond. Hoping that he would not alarm her but needing to get her attention, Robert quickly made up the distance between them and put his hand on her shoulder. The girl made no response but to shrug him off with a small movement and continue on her journey.

"I'm here to help you." Robert called as she moved ever further away from him, "Where are you going?"

"She's going to the Priory." Robert spun around to see where the voice had come from. A small, shrivelled and bent old man sat hunched at the foot of a tree, a ragged blanket around his shoulders. "They all go to the Priory."

"The Priory?" Robert asked, "What Priory?"

"Kirklees." the man replied simply. "Kirklees Priory."

"How do you know?"

"They all go to the Priory."

Kneeling down beside the man, Robert took a few coins from the pouch on his belt and put them into his clawed hand.

"And what of you?" he asked, "Why don't you go?"

"I've been." the man looked distant, "I went to the Priory years ago. When you go. You don't come back."

"What do you mean?" Robert pleaded, sure that this strange statement had something to do with the young man's disappearance. "You came back. You're here."

"No." Said the man stubbornly. "Once you go to the Priory, you don't come back." With that, he turned his head away and closed his eyes. Moments later he was snoring. Frustrated but knowing that he had got all the information he was going to be able to extract from this poor unfortunate, Robert left him and looked along the path for the girl. She was nowhere to be seen.

A sense of urgency and panic rising within him, Robert began to run along the path in the direction she had been walking. She was not there. It was as if she had melted into the rapidly falling darkness.

Stopping to catch his breath, Robert heard a cart trundling along the path behind him. As it drew close he saw that the driver had a hood pulled low over his face, obscuring all but his bearded chin. Sat on the back of the open cart were what appeared to be a family. A man, a woman clutching a baby and three children in ages that ranged from toddler to almost grown. All sat perfectly still and in absolute silence.

"Where are you going?" Robert called. The driver slowed his horse and turned to Robert.

"To the Priory. Everybody goes to the Priory."

"Who are they?" Robert challenged. "Are you taking them against their will?" The driver did not answer but picked up his fairly steady speed once more. "Who is he?" Robert called to the riders, "Why are you going with him?" He began to run behind the cart, easily keeping pace. The woman clutching the baby turned to him and spoke without emotion.

"We're going to the Priory."

"Everybody goes to the Priory." The small boy by her side added.

Making a quick decision, Robert jumped up onto the cart. Neither the riders nor driver challenged him as he sat on the rough wooden bench between two of the older children. No one spoke.

The cart trundled forward, sometimes on the main road through the forest and other times on smaller, twisting paths. After what seemed to be several hours, a pair of huge, imposing iron gates loomed out of the blackness ahead. There seemed to be many people ahead, joining the main road from their many different paths. The main road which lead towards the gates.

"Who are those people?" Robert turned to the girl by his side. "Where is everyone going?"

"They are going to the Priory." She told him flatly. "Everybody goes to the Priory."

"Where is the Priory?" Robert asked, "Is it through those gates?"

"Yes," the Father spoke up in the same strangely dreamlike and emotionless tone as the others. "That is the Priory. We all go to the Priory."

At these strange words, Robert hopped down from the cart which continued to trundle forward. Pulling his hood up over his head, he mixed in with those who were passing through the gates on foot, trying to adopt their same stead, measured gait and pace.

Beyond the gates was a large, imposing building with ornate Gothic towers and windows. A flight of stone steps lead up to heavy oak doors. Everyone seemed to be making their way towards the steps and Robert did likewise.

As the first of the crowd reached the top of the steps, the doors swung open revealing a tall, imposingly beautiful woman standing at the top, dressed in the austere robes of a nun.

"Welcome, my children!" she cooed, "Welcome to the Priory!"

She stepped aside and the people began to enter through the doorway, as if in a trance. Robert stayed with them as best he could as they climbed the steps and filed past the nun who he took to be the Prioress.

"Wait!" she put out a hand, blocking his path, "You are not like the others. I've been expecting you." Robert tried not to register any emotion but she pulled his hood down and turned his face to look at her with her icy hand gripping his chin.

"Oh please," she taunted, "Do you think I don't know who you are? I've had my eye on you for some time, Earl of Loxley."

For a moment, Robert was taken aback to be addressed by the title he had technically inherited upon his Grandfather's death but by which he had never publicly been known. The woman's eyes were dark and soulless. Fearing for his safety and that of those around him, Robert reached for the knife on his belt, only to grasp empty space.

"Come now," the Prioress smirked, "Do you think I'd allow something like that in here? The truth is, everything that passes through those doors belongs to me to do with what I will!"

"Why do you bring these people here?" Robert demanded, seeing the expressionless peasants passing by, paying no attention to the altercation that was taking place right beside them. "What do you want with them?"

"I do not bring them here!" she flared, "They come. Just as you did."

"Just as..." Robert was shocked, "What do you mean?"

"Help my boy, Master Robin!" The Prioress put on a wheedling, pleading voice and as she did so, her form changed to that of the woman who had begged Robert to find her son.

"You tricked me!" cried Robert, "You made me come here!"

"I made you?" the Prioress asked, her form starting to shift once more. "I warned you," she spoke in the form of the old man who had been sleeping by the roadside, "Once you come to the Priory, you don't come back." She shifted once more, becoming the small dark-haired girl. "And yet you came. You came to the Priory! You are mine!"

"Never!" Robert snapped, trying to pull free of her grasp. "I'm leaving and taking as many of these people with me as I can. Then I will come back with men and weapons and destroy you."

"Is that so?" The Prioress took her natural form once more, her voice silky and dangerous. "Do you know what keeps me so beautiful?" She reached out and grabbed a young woman by the tunic and pulled her to her side. The woman made no protest or struggle. "Blood." the Prioress held the young woman's arm out away from her body and ran her sharp fingernail across the forearm so that dark red blood welled up from the wound. "The blood is life." Leaning down, she licked up the sticky red elixir with the tip of her tongue. Robert was repulsed, horrified. He tried to reach out to the young woman, to protect her, but found that he could not move.

Licking her lips, the Prioress raised herself to her full height once more and, with a quick flick of her wrist, broke the young woman's neck. Her body fell to the floor, crumpled and lifeless.

"The blood of the common folk is weak and flavourless." she told Robert, in a tone which was almost conversational. "There are so many of them as to make them worthless. A sip from this one and a mouthful from that one and I am bored. But you, my great hero of noble birth, your blood is powerful and delicious. I plan to savour every last drop."

"So," Robert snarled defiantly, still unable to move to defend himself, "You plan to drain my blood and kill me like you did that girl?"

"Oh no!" the Prioress's mouth formed into a twisted, mirthless smile, "I told you, you are different. A treat like you only comes along once in a generation. I have something very special in mind for you."

Robert was gone. No one knew where. Even Ket and his brother Hob, who usually saw everything that went on in the forest and the surrounding villages and knew more about most people's lives than they did themselves, had no clue.

Knowing that he would not have run away, could not have left her, Holly sat amongst the decaying leaves beneath an oak, dead for the season but with the potential of new life within it, desperately waiting for the thaw when it could be resurrected, and sobbed.

A sound caught her ear. It sounded like someone calling her name, but it was very soft and indistinct. It could have been a rustle in the undergrowth or the breeze whistling through a gap in the branches. She sat up, her senses, supernaturally attuned at the best of times, on high alert, listening for any trace, repeat or echo of the sound. It came again.

"Holly"

This time she was sure she had heard it. What she could not be sure of, however, was where the sound had come from her. Somehow, she felt that it did not originate from the forest around her but from within herself. She waited and she listened. Once more she heard, or rather felt her name being called so clearly it could not be a mistake. There were no further words but she felt drawn to the stream where she always went to think and reflect when things troubled her. She ran through the forest and knelt on a rock, cold as ice from the winter frost, and stared into the water.

At first she saw nothing but her own reflection, peering back at her from the icy flow, but gradually the image changed and distorted, forming itself into something quite different until it was not Holly's own face staring up from the water below, but Robert's!

Peering down into the water, Holly gasped. Robert's image moved his lips and Holly heard his voice yet again. She was sure that her ears were not receiving the sound. Rather, as Robert spoke the words appeared directly in her head.

"Help me!" he cried, hopelessly.

She stretched a hand down into the water, reaching out for him, but the face was just a reflection which shattered as she disturbed the surface of the water. Slowly, it swam back together and re-formed.

"Where are you?" Holly called, desperately hoping that this was just some prank of Robert's, that she would find him hiding in the tree above her head. But deep in her heart she knew this was not true. She listened desperately for an answer, her every sense on heightened alertness, but no reply came and already the face in the water was fading.

"Holly!" Mouthed Robert's face as is melted away leaving only Holly's own reflection staring back up at her, her eyes wide with grief and fear.

Where was her Robert? Why could he not come to her? Why did he need her help?

These thoughts raced through her brain as she swept through the forest to find her father. Like her, he could not leave the forest but he had contacts and allies on the outside. Ket and Hob could find no trace of Robert but someone must have seen him! Men cannot simply disappear like phantoms!

She found him, as he could often be found, sat beneath a tree, playing a sad tune on his flute. Holly knew that he must be thinking of her mother. She held back for a moment before gently touching him on the shoulder. He looked up and smiled at her, but it was a smile of greeting, not of happiness. His eyes betrayed the great sadness he felt, not just at Robert's absence but also the loss of Marian which, although it had occurred so many decades ago in mortal terms, still hurt as if it had happened yesterday. Holly was the one link he had to the all too fleeting time he had spent with his lover, which made her all the more precious. Despite her immortal radiance and elfin features, Holly looked so like her mother.

"I've seen him!" Holly exclaimed. Robin was on his feet immediately. He had no need to ask to whom Holly referred!

"Where?"

"It was only his face, I saw it in the water, but he's trapped somewhere, I know he is, and he needs our help!"

"If he was anywhere in the forest, Ket and Hob would know," Robin mused, "and there's been no word from the travellers through the forest. The death or capture of Robin Hood would certainly be big news!"

At the mention of death, Holly's eyes sprang open even wider than usual with alarm and horror. She had not allowed to herself to entertain the thought that Robert may have been killed, but, try as she might, she could not deny the possibility. Hearing her father speak the words so matter-of-factly had caused the whole concept to be rammed home so that she could not ignore it any more. Robin realised immediately the effect of his words. He put his hands on her shoulders and tried to reassure her.

"Wherever he is," he continued softly, "he has somehow been able to make contact with you. We will find him and we will help him. There is one more person I can ask for help. He is reclusive and prefers to be left alone but in times of dire need, like now, I can call upon his assistance. He has performed services for me in the past and I likewise for him."

Puzzled, Holly wondered who this mysterious person could be. His relationship with her father was clearly long standing, yet she had never heard him spoken of before.

She took her father's hand and they moved through the forest faster than any mortal eye could see. If any human had happened to be watching, it would have seemed as if the pair had simply vanished.

In the blink of an eye, they were standing before what appeared to be a small hillock, covered with twigs, moss and leaves.

"Why are we here?" Holly asked, "There's no one here!"

Smiling a small, private smile, Robin leant forward and tapped on a section of the mound with his knuckles. There was, Holly was more than a little surprised to hear, a hollow sound. A rustling came from inside the hillock and a doorway which had been obscured by the leafy covering swung open, revealing the opening of a dark tunnel. Robin stepped through it and Holly followed close behind.

The tunnel was the entrance to one of the many caves cut from the soft, sandstone ground beneath the forest.

Making their way through the darkness, they came to some steps and followed them down until they came to a wide chamber, filled with strange furniture as would befit a Noble's Manor, dusty charts and works of art hanging on the wall, and books. Lots of books. Stacked on shelves, piled alarmingly high on the floor and littering the many tables and lecterns around the room. Dominating the chamber was a large but simple wooden cross hung from the ceiling. The walls, in between the paintings, embroideries and charts, were adorned with heavy drapes of many different colours and the floor was strewn with exotic rugs from distant lands.

It looked to Holly as if the room were devoid of living inhabitants but Robin called out.

"Tuck!"

There was a shuffling in one corner, and a high-backed chair which was turned away from them was gradually but noisily pushed back. Slowly, as if it caused him great difficulty, an elderly man got to his feet. He wore a simple brown robe, tattered and frayed from countless years of wear, tear and inexpert repair, but Holly saw that his bony finger was adorned with one of her father's rings, the gift that offered his protection in the forest to any who wore it.

Turning to see who had called him, the old man recognised Robin. His face broke into a wide smile and he flung him arms out in greeting. The two men hugged warmly.

"Robin!" exclaimed the man, "My dear, dear friend! It's been so long!"

Robin turned to Holly.

"This," he explained with a warm smile, "is my old friend, Tuck. There was time when he lived in the monastery but that was a long, long time ago. This," he turned to Tuck, "As I'm sure you've realised, is my daughter Holly."

"Of course!" He smiled at Holly who returned the smile but without enthusiasm. Normally she would have been delighted to meet one of her father's mortal friends, to find out about them and their lives, but not today. Her father had promised that, if anyone could help them find and rescue Robert, then it would be this man. Impatient with social niceties, she asked directly;

"Can you help us?"

"Indeed I can," replied Tuck, his face becoming grave, "but remember, sometimes the only way to move beyond pain is to pass through it. Freedom may not take the form we expect and there are worse things than death. I will help you find Robert and release him from his prison. I will do all I can but you, and only you, can set him free."

So taken aback was Holly by these strange, enigmatic words that it took her a few moments to realise that neither of them had mentioned Robert, or anything about the situation in front of this mysterious wise-man. If he knew the problem without having to be told, then perhaps he could be trusted to know the solution as well.

"What must I do?" she asked.

"The Priory at Kirklees." Said Tuck. "Go there. But you must go alone. Only you can bring about his salvation for you love him more than any other. Take this."

Picking up a dusty box from one of the tables the old man opened it with a creak. He took out a small, shiny object which he held out to her. Holly took it and examined it in the palm of her hand.

It was a key. Golden and ornate, with clusters of pale green stones set into both ends. Certainly it was beautiful but Holly could not see how it could help her. It did not look like a dungeon or prison key. Perhaps, she mused silently, it was some kind of magical key which could open any lock. Tuck seemed to know, either by instinct or some unknown power, what she was thinking.

"Just one lock." He informed her solemnly. "Only one lock will it open, and only you can open it. Kirklees Priory. Now," he smiled once more, "I am an old man and I am very tired. Please leave me to my rest."

Warm affection tinged with sadness clearly showing in his eyes, Robin watched as Tuck shuffled back to his seat and settled back down to sleep, then he and Holly turned and made their way back up the sandstone steps out into the forest, Holly still puzzling over the key, now gripped tightly in her fist. Tuck had told her that it would help her to save Robert, but what had he meant by those other things? The strange warnings about pain and the unexpected forms a rescue may take.

"Where is Kirklees Priory?"

"Some way from here. Built within the forest so you should be able to enter it without coming to harm. I can take you to it, but Tuck said you must enter alone."

"Yes I know that's what he said, but why?"

"If I knew the answers to questions of that kind, I should not have needed to consult Tuck in the first place. He is mortal, and he is old, but I have never, in all the years I have known him, ever found him to be wrong about anything."

"Then you mean…"

"If Tuck says you must go alone, then that is what you must do. Only you can set Robert free."

"I'll do anything I have to," stated Holly, boldly, "Show me the Priory."

With a slight flourish, Robin held his palm open flat and, with an intense green glow, his bow appeared. He gripped it with one hand, and with the other he unclipped the bowstring and passed it to Holly. As it left his hand, it lost its ethereal iridescence. Holly threaded it through the top of the key and tied the ends behind her neck, beneath her golden hair, so that the key rested on her chest, over her heart.

Taking her hand, Robin whisked her through the forest until they stood before a pair of imposing, heavy iron gates. The two stood on the rough path which continued beyond the gates.

Peering at the snow-covered grounds beyond, Holly wondered if these gates would be locked, if this would prove to be what the key was for but, after pausing just for a moment to hug her father, she pushed one of the gates and it slowly swung open.

Tentatively, Holly stepped inside, expecting to be challenged, but there was not a soul in sight. Holly considered disguising her appearance, but she had a feeling deep down that any adversary she may face within the priory would not be fooled by the same illusions as mortals. Holly found that humans often helped to deceive themselves by refusing to see anything which contradicted their narrow, but fiercely held world view.

Deserted was not a strong enough word to describe the grounds of the Priory. Not only was there no life to be found, but it seemed as if all the energy, happiness and vitality had been sucked from the area. Holly shivered, and it had nothing to do with the icy winds whistling throughout the forest.

Reaching the ancient oak door of the Priory, Holly wondered what she should do. Would it be best to try to sneak in? A heavy, blackened iron knocker hung just above her eye level. She tried pushing the door but to no avail, and as she could see no other means of entry, she lifted the iron ring and let it fall. The hollow clunk of the metal hitting the wood echoed far beyond the doorway, through the cavernous halls and corridors beyond.

Slowly, as if pulled by unseen hands, the door swung open and Holly stepped inside.

A figure in monk's robes sat on a chair just inside the door. The hood was pulled far down so that Holly could not see his face, but she decided to speak to him. Perhaps someone who actually lived here could explain what she needed to do to get Robert back.

"Hello?" she called, nervously. There was no reply.

Perhaps, Holly thought, the man was sleeping. She tapped him gently on the shoulder. He fell from the chair and collapsed as a heap on the ground. Bones. Old and dry. Holly put her hand to her mouth to stop herself screaming. She ran further inside, seeking someone who could give her answers.

Everywhere there were skeletons. Sat at tables, leant against walls or just crumpled on the floor, nothing more than a pile of dry, lifeless bones from which the human soul was long since departed. Holly ran from room to room but there was not one single living soul.

There was no sign of life anywhere, but Holly could not shake the feeling that she was being watched, by something beyond mortal. A being like herself? No. This presence was malevolent and Holly could feel it's jealously clinging to existence, as if it had no right to a place in the world and continued by trickery, manipulation and evil.

Up ahead was a wide, stone staircase, an oaken door at the top beneath an elaborately carved stone lintel. Holly tentatively put a foot on the steps. A strong wind from nowhere began to blow against her. Bracing herself against the onslaught, Holly slowly climbed. The wind intensified with each step she took. Almost at the top, an unseen force smashed into her, throwing her back to the bottom of the steps.

She hit the stone flags with a jolt that momentarily knocked the breath from her lungs. To a mortal, the fall and impact could well have proved fatal, but Holly stood, ran her fingers through her tangled hair and prepared for a second attempt. This time she would be ready.

After walking a few paces backwards to give herself a good run up, Holly sprinted forward then sprang into a somersault, reaching the top of the steps in two leaps, avoiding the inevitable blow from whatever malign entity obstructed the path of the curious.

At the top of the steps, Holly pushed against the door which swung open without resistance. She stepped through into the room it sealed.

Beyond the door which had slammed shut behind her, Holly found herself in what appeared to be the Priory chapel. The carved stone decorations in the ceiling depicted scenes from the lives of the saints, beautiful except for the faces of each holy figure, which had been chipped away from their heads as if in an effort to eradicate their presence.

Above the altar, where Holly expected to see a wooden cross like the one which hung in Tuck's hermitage, was a cage. And in the cage, Holly realised with a jolt, was Robert!

Rushing to him, Holly put her slender fingers through the bars of the cage, reaching for her beloved. Robert went to take her hands in his but his fingers passed straight through hers. Holly pulled back, shocked.

"I'm getting weaker." Robert told her, his voice cracked and strained, as if he had been screaming for help which never came. "But now you're here! I called out to you and you found me!"

"What has happened to you?" Holly begged, despair welling in her heart.

"Allow me to answer that!" Said a silky voice from behind Holly's shoulder.

Spinning around in alarm, Holly saw a tall woman dressed in a nun's habit facing her. She was beautiful, very beautiful, but her face was cold and hard. There was no human glint behind her deep red eyes. If, indeed, she had ever been human, she had ceased to be a very long time ago.

"What have you done to Robert?" Holly demanded, fury replacing her despair of moments before. "Why can't he touch me?"

The woman's mouth coiled itself into a smile, an evil leer which sent a chill down Holly's spine.

"Precious child," she cooed, "As if he would want to! Do you really believe that someone like him, a man, a hero, could consider you any more than an irritation to be tolerated? A constant nuisance babbling in his ear while he tries to get along with his life?"

"But…" Holly stammered.

"Do you really think such a man could love you? You're a freak! An aberration!"

"Holly!" Robert cried from his cage, "Don't listen to her! I…". The woman swung her arm up sharply, Robert was slammed into the back of the cage and spoke no more.

"You may as well leave! You are nothing to him and he will very soon be nothing to anyone."

Fighting back the tears, Holly knew that this beast in the form of a woman was trying to make her angry, trying to make her doubt Robert and her own feelings, but still her words stung. Holly had seen the young women of the villages surrounding Robert, fawning over their hero and throwing longing looks in his direction. These women were mortal, fully grown and beautiful. How long, Holly had wondered time and time again, would it be before Robert took a mortal wife, a woman he could love, grow old with and raise a family, leaving Holly all alone for the rest of her immortal existence.

To Holly, the woman's evil was plain, but would Robert, a mortal man, have seen it? Could he have been blinded by her beauty and seduced away from Holly with the promise of a love of the kind he could not share with the immortal nymph?

"What's the matter, little girl?" the woman taunted. "Afraid that your precious man loves me more than you?"

"Never!" Holly spat back with contempt. "Now tell me what you've done to him! Why did his hands pass through mine! He's..."

"Gone, my dear! A dead man!"

"But I can see him! I spoke to him!"

"Indeed you did, my dear! When you came in, in fact! You were kind enough to help him to the floor!"

"No!" cried Holly, remembering the skeletal heap by the door. Surely not! Surely that could not have been her precious Robert! "Robert's alive! He spoke to me!"

"Oh come now, my little darling", the woman spoke softly. A dangerous sound. "You should know as well as anyone that a spirit can live on beyond the mortal body!"

"Well, yes," Holly admitted shakily, "But why is he still here?"

"For me!" The woman exclaimed, "To feed me! To keep me young and beautiful forever!"

With a sickening lurch, Holly understood. This foul creature, this parasite, fed off the life force of others. She was slowly consuming Robert's soul and would continue until he was gone forever, swallowed up in her evil being.

Suddenly Tuck's admonitions made sense. Certainly there were worse things than physical death. She had to stop this. She had to set Robert free!

"How?" She demanded, "How do you leach his energy from him? How can you consume a human soul?"

The woman lowered her face so that her eyes were level with Holly's. She could smell her foul, foetid breath. Up close, her beauty seemed false, mask-like. Her deep red eyes flashed with evil.

"Blood, my precious little one, the blood is the life!"

She wafted her hand towards the altar. There was a deep rumble and a heavy scratching sound as a stone panel from the front rotated. On a shelf on the reverse of the panel stood a gold, jewel-encrusted goblet. Turning towards Holly, she took a swipe at the girl, knocking her to the ground.

Sweeping majestically forward, the woman seized the goblet and swallowed a draft from it. A trickle of sticky, red liquid began to dribble from the side of her mouth. She gathered it up on the tip of her finger which she licked, sensuously.

"Not one precious drop must be wasted." She informed the stricken Holly who was still lying on the stone floor, her stomach knotted with horror and disgust.

Looking over to where Robert lay, crumpled in his cage, Holly saw with horror that he appeared somehow diminished. Less distinct. When the Prioress had consumed his blood, it was his life-force that she absorbed. She clambered unsteadily to her feet.

"It's too late, sweet child, you cannot save him! One more mouthful, just one more sip, and your precious hero shall be gone!"

Suddenly, Holly realised what she must do.

As the Prioress flung her head back and laughed her evil, triumphant cackle, Holly leapt forward, twisting in the air so as to catch the demon unawares. She grabbed the goblet from her unwary hand, careful not to let even one drop fall to the ground. With her impeccable agility and balance, keeping the goblet level, Holly sprung towards Robert's cage, landing on the top.

Within the cage, Robert lay unconscious, his head lolled backwards and his already spectral form becoming ever fainter. Holly paused. If she was wrong, if her theory proved false, the Robert was doomed. Yet if she did nothing, Robert would be doomed for certain. If this worked, then there was still a chance. Robert's mortal life was passed. Nothing could be done to alter that, and she would mourn him when he was gone and forever after, but if she could save his soul from the terrible fate this creature had in store, then she must try.

Carefully, Holly tilted the goblet so that the thick, rich, life-infused red liquid poured through the bars of the cage into Robert's unconscious, open mouth. It did not pass through him.

Robert's eyes sprung open. Re-energised and alive! He stood up straight, without any weakness or unsteadiness. He reached up towards Holly, touching her outstretched fingers with his own.

For a moment, the Prioress's eyes widened with alarm but her face quickly sunk back to its customary mocking scorn.

"A valiant try, my darling, but pointless. His life is over. He will fade as he did before and be lost to you. I shall find another to nourish me, as I have taken so many before!"

Nimbly, Holly climbed down the cage and rattled the door. It was locked tight. Frustrated and desperate, Holly shook the door violently and tried to tear it from its hinges. Unable to budge it even slightly, Holly smacked impotently at it with the palms of her hands before slumping backwards, bitter tears of anger, frustration and grief stinging her eyes.

"It's okay, my love," Robert spoke softly from within the cage, reaching out to her as best he could. "You did all that you could. If this is the end of my existence then all that matters is that I got to see you one final time."

"No!" Holly protested angrily as the Prioress smirked, "It can't end this way! It just can't!" She looked pleadingly at Robert. "Tuck said if anyone could help you, I could! There has to be a way! I have to find..."

Out of the corner of her eye, she saw another object on the plinth where the goblet had stood. A key.

Triumphantly, grinning excitedly at Robert, she grabbed it and thrust it into the lock. Instantly, it began to glow, becoming white hot in her hand, forcing her to release her grip.

"I told you," smirked the Prioress as Holly looked imploringly at Robert, "There is nothing to be done! That cage is sealed with the power of an evil far greater than you could ever hope to match!"

As the beast spoke, Tuck's words flashed through Holly's mind.

"Only you can bring about his salvation for you love him more than any other."

In that instant, Holly understood why the Prioress had tried so hard to make her angry. To make her doubt Robert and her own feelings. This was the demon's one weakness.

Suddenly aware of the cool metal against her skin, Holly remembered the key which hung around her neck. It was not the same size as the one which sat in the lock, it was much smaller. Surely this could not be the answer? But she had to believe, had to try.

Ripping the heavy key from the hole, she thrust in her own key and turned it. At first, nothing happened. Then the bars began to glow with a soft green light.

"No!" Screamed the Prioress, rushing wildly towards Holly. But now it was her turn to be repelled by an unseen force. She cowered, her arm covering her face in a feeble, child like attempt at self-preservation.

The glowing cage melted like ice placed before a fire, leaving Robert standing proud and tall on the altar. He leapt down and stood beside Holly.

"Love," declared Holly, folding her arms defiantly, "is more powerful than any evil."

Taking a few steps forward, Robert held out his right arm and, to Holly's amazement, a bow appeared as she had seen so many times in her father's hand. Robert pulled back the bowstring, letting fly a flaming green arrow which struck the Prioress clean through the heart.

Nothing could have prepared Holly for what happened next.

Her eyes blazing red, the Prioress's darkly beautiful face froze in an expression of abject horror. Her eyes dulled as the skin around them began to wrinkle and pucker. Within seconds she was a wizened, bent old woman. But the process did not stop there! Her desiccated flesh fell away leaving only a grotesquely grinning skeleton which crumbled before their eyes.

A shriek arose from the heap of dust and bone fragments, but it was not a sound of horror or torture, it was the sound of countless thousands of souls crying with joy as they were released from their hellish imprisonment.

For an instant, the room was full of men, women and children. All laughing with joy and relief. But in the blink of an eye they had gone, and Robert and Holly were left alone.

Robert grabbed Holly by the hand.

"Quick!" he cried, "I don't have much time left!"

They ran to the entrance of the priory, where the crumpled skeleton lay by the door. Robert scooped up the bundle that had been his mortal body and stepped out into the sunlight. He placed the bundle at his feet, raising his hand above his eyes to deflect the glare from the low sun.

All around them, life was returning to the grounds of the abbey. A red-breasted robin settled in the branches of one of the trees and a hare hopped tentatively through the bars of the gate, leaving its distinctive prints in the snow. The browned leaves of a holly bush became suffused with deep, living green and bright red berries sprouted instantly.

"I do not have much time." Robert repeated, holding out a hand in front of his face. Already it was starting to fade. His time in the mortal world was over. He knew it. Imbibing the blood had restored his soul to him but not his body. That was gone, now no more than a heap of bones and nothing could restore it.

Stretching out his mystical bow once more, Robert let fly a final arrow which disappeared beyond the horizon.

"Bury my remains where the arrow lands."

Holly could not speak. The tears were pouring down her elfin face and words stuck in her throat. Another voice spoke from behind her. A gentle but commanding voice. Her father.

"You have done well, my children." He said, softly. "Now the time is near for you, Robert, to leave this world, but I would not have you go without a farewell. If ever a mortal was worthy to carry my name, it is you. We will meet again, brother."

As Robin held out his hand, Robert took it to shake but Robin pulled him into an embrace. Warmly, the pair hugged each other. Robin stepped back and gave a theatrical bow, a gesture which Robert returned, a grin on his face.

"And now," Robin smiled a sideways smile which was ever so nearly a smirk, "I think there's someone else who needs your time a little more urgently than I do." With a final nod to his apprentice, Robin faded and was gone.

At first, neither Robert nor Holly spoke. They simply looked at each other. Holly seemed uncertain.

"It really is me." Robert held out his hands to her and she took them, still solid despite their translucency. His skin felt warm and alive. Looking up at him, Holly ran her hand gently over his face. It felt as it had always done, and yet now it was different. He was different. "I don't belong here any more." he told her, softly. "I cannot stay."

"But why?" Holly pleaded, her large brown eyes filled with tears. "Stay with me! I need you!" She sobbed. "I love you!"

"There's nothing I want more than that." Robert assured her, cupping her elfin face in his hands and brushing away the tears with his thumbs. "I don't want to be apart from you for even a single moment."

Desperately, Holly flung her arms around her beloved, clinging tightly to him as if by doing so she could hold him there forever, anchoring him in the world of the living.

Hot tears formed in Robert's eyes which had taken on a green glow like Robin's, rolling down his cheeks and falling into Holly's golden hair and he held her close, his arms tightly wrapped around her shoulders and his fingers in her hair.

Realising that he had only a few moments left, Robert knelt so that his face was level with Holly's.

"I love you," she whispered. "Always and forever."

"I love you too." Robert assured her. "Now I have to go. I don't want to. Oh my love, please believe me when I say I want nothing more than to stay here with you but I know I must go." He pulled her close and kissed her tenderly. "It is a good place," he told her, "that place where I am going."

"I want to come too!" Holly begged. "Can't I, Robert? Can't I come with you?"

"Not yet," Robert stroked her hair soothingly, "The time is not yet right but I shall wait for you there, preparing a place for you by my side until it is time for you to join me."

"When will that be?" Holly pleaded, "A single minute in a world without you is too long!"

"I shall never leave your heart," Robert placed his hand gently on Holly's chest, feeling the beat of her heart, "and you shall never be absent from mine, not even for a moment. We will be together again, my love. I promise you."

Feeling as if the grief would kill her and wishing it could be so, Holly entwined her fingers in Robert's hair and pulled him towards her, closing her eyes and kissing him, gently at first and then with the passion of one who knows she must soon be parted from the one she loves.

His strong arms around her, Holly felt Robert grow warmer and his physical form less solid. She tried to hold on tight but her arms passed through him, wrapping themselves around her own shoulders. Her eyes still closed, Holly felt surrounded by a warm cloud of love, as if her Robert was all around her.

Opening her eyes, she saw the last green wisps of mist fading smoke on the breeze. In a few moments more he was gone, leaving only the warmth of the kiss against her lips.

Slumping down on her knees, Holly burst into loud, angry, uncontrollable tears. She sobbed until she had no more tears left. Robert was gone.

When the time was right, she and Robin gathered up Robert's mortal remains and buried them where the arrow had landed. They placed a stone over the place where he lay and Holly inscribed a final epitaph for her beloved friend.

In the centuries that followed, the words would fade, to be repaired and replaced by people who knew only the legend, but not the man. These are the true words which Holly wrote:

**Here beneath this little stone
Lies Robert, for his soul has flown
No archer as he was so good
And people called him Robin Hood
The like of he, this finest of men
Shall England never see again**

Raven

The frosts were melting. Slowly the creatures of the forest emerged from their hibernation. The trees, left bare by the harsh winter winds, began to sprout new, green leaves and their branches sprouted forth beautiful blossoms. After the cruel and baron winter, life was returning to the forest but Holly's spirits were not lifted by the beauty she saw around her.

Robert was gone. Murdered by the Prioress of Kirklees. His short life of heroism and bravery had been rewarded by an ignominious death at the hands of a servant of the Dark Spirit. Holly's heart ached when she thought of him, pictured his face calling to her from the water, remembered the happy hours, days and months they had spent together, too swiftly cut short.

Many things he had been to her, and she to him, but most importantly he had been her friend. The one mortal she had ever felt such a strong connection to, as if their souls were meant to be together, as if they were the missing piece of each other. She had never felt more herself than when she was with Robert. And he was gone.

Although Holly knew in her heart that he was now in a place far beyond the darkness that was the mortal world with its pain, suffering and death, this knowledge was of little consolation. Her heart screamed that his place was there with her, by her side. She tried to picture him in the Eternal Forest. She had seen that place with her own eyes. She had met her mother there more than an entire mortal lifetime ago. Learned the truth that the physical world she now occupied, with all its apparent permanence and grandeur was but a fleeting shadow, an imperfect echo of the Eternal Forest which existed before time, after time and all around it. Eternal, unchanging and tangibly alive. She knew that he was with his family and her mother, safe and peaceful, but she wanted him there with her and could not imagine how he could be truly happy without her. She missed him as if her very soul had been torn in half.

For months, Holly had avoided the parts of the forest where the mortals travelled. She had always loved watching them secretly as they went about their business, but that was before. Now she preferred to stay in the deep, dark, inaccessible parts of the forest where no mortal had ever set foot, where her company was the elves, fairies and other greenwood spirits.

Consumed by her grief, Holly was sitting at the foot of a mighty oak tree, it's ancient and gnarled branches stretching out majestically like a conductor leading the orchestra. Her knees were tucked up under her chin and her eyes, glazed and staring, pointed in the direction of a small, bright green fern growing from the mulch of last years' leaves which decayed steadily around the tree, renewing the ground and allowing new life to spring from the remnants of the old. Looking towards it, but not at it. She may as well have been starring at a rock or a fallen branch. She didn't care any more. How long had she been sitting there? An hour? Two? The passing of days, with their promise of hope and fresh chances, seemed irrelevant, pointless.

Suddenly there was a great crashing through the undergrowth and an enormous dog bounded towards her. Holly jumped up with a start but the dog stopped in from of her, wagging his tail and barking affectionately.

She knelt down and buried her fingers in the shaggy grey fur behind his ears. He licked her cheek and she giggled.

"Well," she said, smiling for the first time in months, "you're a handsome fellow. Where did you come from?"

The hound pricked up his ears and looked back towards the broken vegetation he'd just burst through. Her hearing only slightly less sensitive than his, Holly almost immediately heard the voice. It was a high, soft voice. A human voice. Hearing the speaker coming closer, Holly blended her appearance with the tree and waited.

The undergrowth parted and Holly was surprised to see a human girl emerge. She was smaller than Holly, about eight years old, her hair long, black and tangled. Her dark eyes sparkling as she looked around for her faithful companion.

"Ah, there you are!" she cried out happily, pausing to unhook her tunic from where it had become snagged on a thorn. The dog ran towards her enthusiastically. Holly's curiosity got the better of her. She allowed the girl to see her.

"Oh, hello" Said the girl, looking up with a start. "I'm sorry, I didn't see you there! I hope he hasn't been bothering you?"

"Not at all," replied Holly. "What's his name?"

"Well, his name's Wolf but I tend to call him 'Useless'" She scratched the top of his head with the tips of her fingers and he panted contentedly.

"Useless?"

"He's meant to be a hunting dog but he's about as savage as a dead hedgehog!"

Standing up, the girl brushed the dog hair and leaves off the front of her tunic and held out her hand.

With surprise, Holly noticed the ring on the girl's finger, a delicate silver ring set with a shimmering green stone. One of her father's rings. The rings he gave to those who were under his protection.

She was sure that her father would have told her if he had met this girl, but he had said nothing. And yet, clearly, the ring on her finger had come from him.

Sure the explanation would be made clear in due time., Holly resolved not to ask about it.

"I'm Raven." Announced the girl. Holly shook her hand, amused at the formality, and told the girl her name.

They were a long way from the safe path that most people took and Holly wondered what Raven was doing this deep in the forest. Holly knew that human parents told their children terrifying stories of what could happen to them if they were to stray from the path, that was why it seemed strange to find such a young girl out on her own so far into the secret greenwood that only Holly and her family knew. Perhaps the ring had been a direct gift from her father after all?

"I hope you don't mind me asking," enquired Holly, politely, "but what are you doing all the way out here on your own? Surely you know it's dangerous?"

Tossing her hair nonchalantly, Raven gave Holly a confident smile.

"My father's one of the King's foresters! He's paid to live here and stop the outlaws from poaching the King's deer."

At that point, Holly had to suppress a giggle. She had yet to see a forester stop any determined poacher, and she had seen a fair few of these hired men get themselves hopelessly lost or worse, even after they'd been working in the forest for years.

What they often failed to understand was that the forest is not like a building, it does not stay the same year after year after year. It is a living entity, made up of the hundreds of thousands of organisms within it. Constantly growing; constantly evolving; constantly changing.

Many was the time Holly had had to help her father rescue these unfortunate fellows before they died from hunger or exposure.

"I've lived in this forest since I was two," continued Raven, "and there's not a patch of it I don't know!"

Not wanting to knock her new acquaintance's confidence, Holly decided not to point out the obvious untruth of what she said. After all, Holly had never seen her before so she can't have been familiar with the whole forest! Although, Holly reflected, she may well believe she was telling the truth, as there were parts of the forest that she knew no mortal had ever seen and, probably, ever could!

Narrowing her eyes suddenly, Raven looked intently at Holly.

"Anyway," she asked, slowly, "I could ask you the same question! You might be a bit older than me but you're certainly no grown-up! What are you doing out here on your own? You don't even have a dog!"

"I thought you said he was useless?"

"He is, but the robbers don't know that do they? All they see is a very big dog! Anyway, stop trying to change the subject and answer the question!"

"Oh, my father's..." Holly paused, realising that Raven probably wouldn't believe the truth even if she told her, "He works in the forest too!"

Squatting down again, Raven was tickling her affectionate hound behind the ears. Holly joined her. Raven looked up to the sky where the sun was just visible through the thick branches of the trees. It was late afternoon and would be starting to get dark soon.

"I'd better be heading back to my cottage," said Raven, "Or Father will be starting to wonder where I am!" She paused for a moment then, Holly was surprised to see, looked a little embarrassed.

"What's wrong?" asked Holly.

"Oh, nothing's wrong" Raven replied hurriedly, "I was just wondering if you would like to come back with me and meet my father. You could stay for the night if you wanted?"

A thousand conflicting thoughts burst simultaneously into Holly's mind. She could not deny that she liked this girl, or that she was lonely and desperately wanted a friend, but could she risk it? Could she allow herself to be close to another mortal? Could she bear to see another friend die?

Raven was looking at her, her large dark eyes filled with expectation and, Holly could see very clearly, a terrible loneliness. Holly knew what it was like to be alone, to be the only one of her kind. She could imagine how alone Raven must feel, a mortal girl alone in the forest with only her father and dog for company. Holly had no doubt that Raven loved her father, as she did her own, and the dog was clearly a faithful and loving companion but neither were any substitute for a friend; someone you could share your heart and soul with; someone who made the world feel just that little bit less terrifying; someone like Robert.

The thought of Robert brought a tear to Holly's eye but she blinked it out quickly, hoping that Raven hadn't noticed. Her heart ached. She closed her eyes for a moment and saw Robert's face behind her eyelids. He smiled at her and she understood.

She understood that Robert, who had lost so much in his short life, had never lost the ability to love again. His parents and his grandparents, everyone he had ever loved, had been cruelly taken from him by disease or evil action, yet he had still been able to love her father as a brother and mentor. And he had loved her.

In an instant she made up her mind.

"That would be lovely!" she said. Raven's face lit up with an excited smile.

"Do you need to tell your family where you're going?" she asked.

Once again, Holly smiled to herself. It was highly unlikely that she could go anywhere in the forest without her family knowing! If Ket or Hob weren't watching from the undergrowth then the tree spirits were sure to see her. Only once had she been beyond their sight. Outside of their world to a different world. The world where she had met her mother. The world where Robert now existed.

"No, that should be fine!" she replied cheerfully, taking Raven's hand, and, with the faithful hound by their side, they set off back through the trampled undergrowth to Raven's cottage.

It was a strange little place. Not at all like the cottages that Holly had seen in the village. It was in the middle of an artificial clearing and was built entirely from materials gathered from the surrounding forest.

Its circular walls were made from sawn logs thrust deep into the ground, with clay-like mud, dried rock solid, packed between them. The roof was woven from supple branches and had various trails of ivy and honeysuckle growing through it. There was no front door but the entrance was covered by a heavy leather curtain.

At the sound of the girls' voices and the happy yelping of the dog, a large hand pushed the curtain aside and out walked the tallest mortal man Holly had ever seen. True, he was not as tall as John, that would be impossible, but he was much taller than any of the other foresters, traders or passing beggars she had ever seen. His grey hair was thick and tangled, like his daughter's, and hung untidily around his shoulders. The lower portion of his face was covered by a thick, but shortly cropped beard.

He flung his arms out wide with a huge welcoming smile and Raven rushed towards him. Her little arms would not reach all the way around his waist but he wrapped his round her and lifted her off the ground with a great bear hug. She shrieked with delight. He put her down and turned to smile at Holly.

"Who's your friend?" he asked, ruffling Raven's hair.

"This is Holly," she replied. "She lives in the forest too. Her father works here like you!"

Over the years, Holly had become used to humans not noticing her and, when they did, they tended just to see a normal girl. They failed to notice the pointed ears, the slightly too large eyes and the golden sheen of her skin. She had long ago come to realise that mortals only saw what they wanted or expected to see. Anything that would challenge their perception of reality, they would conveniently fail to notice.

But Raven's father seemed different. When he looked at her, Holly had the feeling that he could see her as she truly was. And yet he did not seem alarmed by her. After a short pause where he seemed to be gathering his thoughts, he smiled again and said;

"Of course! I know him well. Come in! Come in!"

He held aside the curtain and ushered the girls inside. Holly gasped as she took in the interior of the hut.

The walls had been coated with the same clay that had been used to plug the gaps on the outside. In a couple of places near the floor where the clay had fallen away, Holly could see that they were lined with young branches woven together like a fence before being covered in the smooth clay. The clay had then been covered with a layer of lime to whiten them but the walls were hung with vivid embroideries showing, to Holly's amazement, images of her father! In one he was shown taking aim with his trusty bow, in another he was shown blowing a horn to summon his men, another showed him protectively holding the shoulder of a small, dark-haired girl that Holly took to be Raven, in the next he stood with Marian under a spreading oak tree and in the last, Holly saw with a start, he held a small golden baby in his arms.

The man was looking carefully at Holly, trying to gauge her reaction to the images. Holly felt instinctively that this man could be trusted but she didn't want to discuss her father in front of Raven. After all, despite what Holly had originally suspected when she saw the ring, Raven hadn't realised that there was anything unusual about Holly and apparently thought she was just another girl who happened to live nearby, a girl with whom she could be friends, and Holly wanted to keep it that way for the time being at least.

The pressed-earth floor was strewn with reed mats. Two beds, small but beautifully carved from oak, stood to one side, opposite an equally beautiful oak table around which were a number of simple wooden stools. Raven's father took three of these and stood them around the fireplace where a small but warm fire crackled happily under a blackened copper pot.

"Hope you don't mind if I get on with cooking while you two talk?" asked the man, "Only, it's been a busy day and I expect everyone's hungry!"

Next to the fire there was a barrel of freshly dug vegetables. He brushed most of the dried mud off with his hands then chucked some of them into the already bubbling pot. He then took down a lump of venison from a hook on the ceiling and dropped that in too. He then took his seat by the fire with the girls and absent-mindedly stirred the pot, pausing every now and then to join in their conversation. When the meal was ready he took three wooden bowls from the mantle-piece and spooned the delicious-smelling stew into each of them.

Like most of the greenwood folk, Holly did not actually need to eat but she liked to when she could. She loved the tastes, smells and textures of mortal food and greatly enjoyed eating this meal with her new friends.

After they had eaten, they played a game where each of them in turn pretended to be a particular forest animal while the others tried to guess what they were. Unsurprisingly, Holly was the best at it but Raven and her father had a fair amount of talent themselves, Raven's best impersonation being that of a wolf, complete with sound effects, and by the end of the game all three were laughing until the tears ran down their faces. The dog, having helped himself to the rest of the stew while nobody was watching, joined in the game by providing uncannily timed growls and howls which made the impression all the funnier!

As it was now night time and rather cold outside, the man built up the fire and they sat around it again. It was not long before Raven's head began to loll to the side. She was struggling to keep her eyes open and in no time at all she was fast asleep. Her father picked her up gently and carried her over to one of the beds. He set her down, pulled her grubby tunic over her head and covered her with the warm blanket. The dog jumped up on the bed and settled himself to sleep by her feet.

"I should probably be going." Said Holly, standing up and heading towards the door. "Thank you for a lovely evening. I hope I can come back again some time!"

"Of course, you're always welcome." Said the man, as he dropped Raven's tunic into a barrel and took another from the shelf which he then folded in half and hung over the end of Raven's bed, ready for the morning. "After all, Raven and I owe our very existence to your father!"

Upon hearing this surprising observation, Holly's curiosity got the better of her. She had not wanted to talk about her father in front of Raven but she was now asleep, with the dog, snoring contentedly, flopped across her feet. She had to know how this man knew of her father, where the strange pictures had come from and why he owed his life to him.

The man smiled, obviously sensing Holly's questions before she had any need to ask them.

"Sit down, if you'd like to, and I'll tell you about my mother."

This surprised Holly a little as it was her father they had been talking about rather than this man's mother. But she desperately wanted to know what he had to tell her so she sat back down on the stool by the fire.

"How old are you?" he asked Holly, who pondered for a moment before replying.

"It's difficult to know for sure," she said, "but I think I was born about sixty summers ago."

The man nodded.

"Yes," he replied, "That would be about right. You see, I'm a similar age myself, a little less perhaps. Raven's my youngest daughter but I have other children. They're all grown up now with families of their own. Anyway, a few years before you were born, my mother met your father."

He went over to his own bed and felt around under the pillow. He pulled something out but it was obscured by his big hand and Holly could not see what it was.

"When my mother was a little girl, not much older than Raven is now, she went to the market for her mother. There was nothing particularly unusual about this, she went at least once a month, but on this occasion she found this."

He held out his hand and slowly opened it. Holly saw a small, crudely carved wooden figure, made to look all the smaller by his wide palm. It was the figure of a bearded man. The paintwork was scuffed and worn with age but his tunic was still clearly coloured green, as were his vivid, almost too lifelike eyes. It was unmistakeably a model of her father. Holly gasped.

"And that's not all," the man continued, "on her way home, ignoring the warnings of her parents and all others she met, she strayed from the path and found herself lost in the forest.

She was set upon by a group of savage outlaws who tried to kill her and take what little money and goods she had with her. She was sure that she was going to die but then…"

He paused and Holly was almost certain what was coming next. She had heard stories like this before.

"But then, a mysterious man in green appeared. He shot her attackers with arrows which seemed to be made from pure light and faded away to nothing leaving no mark at all. It was the man depicted by the model she carried. Your father."

This thought brought a smile to Holly's face. She was always pleased to hear stories of her father's heroic exploits.

"After he saved her, he took her safely home. To this very cottage in fact. She never saw him again but she never forgot him. He had left her a ring which she wore until the day she died, the ring Raven now wears, although she doesn't understand its significance. Over the years she heard people telling stories about him and would tell them her own. She knew your mother too. They had been friends when they were very young and saw each other from time to time. When Marion disappeared, my mother knew where she must have gone.

She was delighted when she heard from a travelling minstrel that you had been born. She always hoped one day to catch a glimpse of you but she never did. Still, she'd be delighted to know that you were friends with her granddaughter!

She spent the last few years of her life stitching the pictures you can see around the walls, they were her tribute to the man who'd saved her life."

He pointed to the picture of Robin with the dark haired girl.

"That's her in that picture there. Doesn't Raven look like her? Anyway, so now you see that Raven and I owe our lives to your father. If he hadn't rescued her when she was a girl then we wouldn't be here today."

He stood up and walked to the doorway and pulled aside the curtain.

"It's very late," he said, "You'd be welcome to stay for the night. You can have my bed, I can sleep by the fire. It's quite comfortable really!"

"If you're sure it's no trouble?" Holly asked. He gave another of his great beaming smiles.

"None whatsoever!"

Gratefully, Holly tucked herself under the blankets of the second bed and before she knew it she was fast asleep. She dreamt of her father and the girl with the black hair, of how he had rescued her from the forest bandits, how it was because of him that her new friends were alive.

As she awoke, the early morning sun was bursting in through the tiny holes in the ceiling, dappling everything in the cottage with spots of light like the forest floor when the sun shone through the dense canopy of the trees.

The dog barked happily as he tried to catch the twinkling dabs of light with his paw, clearly a game he enjoyed most mornings. Raven's father was nowhere to be seen. He had obviously already gone out into the forest for his day's work. Raven was standing by Holly's bed, shaking her shoulder rather violently.

"Holly!" She called, not particularly quietly. "Holly, are you awake?"

Holly sat up.

"Well I certainly am now!" She smiled at her friend. Raven jumped in next to her and pulled the warm blanket round her shoulders.

"Do you like the pictures?" Raven asked, "My Grandma made them before she died. She was obsessed with Robin Hood. She said she'd met him when she was a girl but I know that can't be right! I saw him last year when he won the silver arrow and he wasn't much more than twenty so how could she have known him when she was little? He'd have to be a hundred years old!"

A pang of sadness struck Holly's heart. Clearly the Robin Hood that Raven had seen was Robert, her precious Robert. She knew Raven didn't mean to upset her but she didn't want to talk about Robert. She knew her father's legend had been around long before even she was born.

"Well," she said, smiling cheekily at Raven, "perhaps he just doesn't get old?"

The small girl looked thoughtful for a moment.

"I wish I didn't have to get old." She said, sadly. "Grandma got old then she died. Even Father is getting old even though he's still stronger than any other man in the forest. If only I could stay a girl."

Now it was Holly's turn to look thoughtful. She was an eternal child. She knew that even if she lived for a thousand years she would never look any older than she did now. She also knew that everyone else around her would get old. Any mortal friend she made would get older and older until they died. Or worse, like Robert, their life would be cut short before they ever had the chance to grow old. She wished that her new friend could stay the way she was, stay young with her forever. Yet she knew that was impossible.

"Come on!" cried Raven, suddenly, "We can't stay in bed all day! We need to take old Useless out for a run before he gets bored and starts to tear everything up!"

Looking over, Holly saw that the hound had already started chewing the corner of one of the reed mats on the floor, and not for the first time either to judge by the state of it!

The girls hopped out of the snug bed. Raven pulled on the fresh tunic and ran her fingers through her hair to untangle the worst of the knots then, holding back the leather door curtain, she whistled to the dog who ran out happily, excited, as most dogs are every morning, by the prospect of a new adventure.

Holly followed the pair outside.

They say that time has no meaning when you are happy. The days Holly spent with Raven, her father and her excitable hound seemed to stretch on forever.

Through the height of the summer, the two girls roamed the forest, faithful hound in tow. Together they explored the hidden corners normally unseen by travellers who pass through without actually seeing the beauty that surrounded them.

For Holly, Raven's wonder at each new discovery was truly inspirational. She felt as if she too were seeing these wonders for the first time. In the evenings they would sit by the hearth with Raven's father and share stories, or tales of their day's adventures.

Like so many things that seem perfect, however, this utopian existence was not to last.

The day started like so many others. Holly arrived at the cottage just as the man was leaving for his day's work. They exchanged smiles and he playfully ruffled Holly's hair as she passed.

As she often had to, Holly shook Raven out of bed and the three of them, dog included, headed off into the forest to see what new excitements the day would bring.

Happily, they romped together as the morning gave way to midday. They chased each other between the trees and swam in the stream, getting showered repeatedly as they tried to dry themselves in the sun by the dog who kept insisting on diving into the crystal water then leaping out and shaking himself off.

As the light began to wane, the girls headed back to the cottage. As they approached the clearing, the dog began to bark. Not a happy or excited bark this time but a bark of distress – he clearly knew that something was wrong!

He bounded forward, leaving the leather curtain flapping madly. Raven was next, with Holly close behind her. The sight that met Holly's eyes as she burst through the curtain, had she been mortal, would have been enough to make her heart stop. Raven's father was lying on the floor in front of the fireplace with the dog nuzzling around his head, trying to push him up with his nose. Raven was on her knees next to his chest, calling out to him, begging him to wake up. But Holly knew.

Even if she had not been able to feel when the spark of life had left a body, if she had just been a normal girl like Raven, she would have known. He was lying on the floor but he did not look like he was lying down to sleep. Rather, he looked empty, almost like a heap of cloths discarded by their wearer. The part of him which had made him who he was had gone, leaving just an empty shell.

Running to her friend, Holly put her arms around her shoulders. Raven buried her face in Holly's hair and cried uncontrollably. Holly knew where that man had gone. Knew that he was now reunited with his mother and his wife. Her heart let out a silent call to Robert and to her mother to take care of him. She held Raven very tight until the small girl had cried herself to sleep. Then, as her father had done, she carried her over to her bed and tucked her under the warm blankets. Raven's faithful hound took his customary place at the foot of her bed and closed his eyes but this time he slept deeply. There was no snoring.

For some time, Holly sat by the man's body and looked at him. He seemed so peaceful. A log had fallen by his right hand. He had clearly been building up the fire ready to cook an evening meal when his heart had given way and his spirit had left his body. She leant over and gave him a gentle kiss on the forehead. He had, after all, if only for a very short time, been her friend.

She knew that Raven was too young to live on her own. Her father had mentioned other children who were now adult. Holly was sure that one of them would take her in. Tomorrow morning, she decided, she would go with Raven to the edge of the forest, as far as she dare go, and trust that someone in the village would be able to help her.

She looked again at the body. It was important that Raven should be able to say goodbye to her father but she also knew that she would not be able to make funeral arrangements on her own. She quietly left the cottage, stood by the edge of the trees and called out to her father.

Silently, with a gentle breeze, Robin appeared. Holly flung her arms around him. Sometimes it would be days or even weeks between the times they saw each other but they were as close as a father and daughter can be. Closer, in fact, as they had been together longer.

"Why?" she asked, sobbing. "Why did he go? Raven's just a little girl! She needs her father!"

Looking at his daughter's dark, tear-filled eyes, Robin knew that it was not just the loss of Raven's father that was distressing her. The tragedy had opened the wound for her which had only just been beginning to heal. He smiled a kind, gentle smile and brushed the hair from her face.

"But she had him for a while." he said gently. "There are many children born into this world who never know the love of a mother or a father. She had him for nearly nine years, and his other children for longer. Now she will go and live with one of her brothers or sisters. She will have a new family that will love her. Then one day she'll have a family of her own that she will love because she's been shown such love. Just as you were. One moment of love would be worth a lifetime of loneliness, but no one ever need be lonely. A heart that knows how to love will never be alone."

The bitter tears stinging her eyes, Holly pulled him tighter to her. She knew that he could not feel physical sensation as mortals do, like she did, but his spectral form felt warm against her face and she was glad of his comforting presence.

Following close behind Holly, Robin entered the house and formed a blanket of leaves in his hands which he lay gently over the body. He then sat down with his back against the wall and Holly climbed into his lap. He wrapped his cloak around both of them and Holly fell into a gentle, dreamless sleep.

In the morning, Holly stretched and walked quietly over to Raven's bed. The dog had moved around during the night and now lay beside her with his head on her pillow. She was snuggled up to him, cuddling him like an enormous stuffed toy. She looked so young and vulnerable lying there asleep. Holly could hardly bear to wake her up, to bring her back to this world of pain and sadness but she knew that she must. She reached out and touched her gently on the arm.

Murmuring slightly, Raven opened her eyes. The dog jumped down off the bed and went to investigate the stranger in the green cloak standing silently in the corner. Robin knelt down and tickled the dog behind the ears.

As she rubbed her eyes and blinked a few times, it took Raven a moment to remember why Holly was there and what had happened the night before. Her large eyes filled with tears again and Holly sat down next to her.

"Who's that?" Raven asked, pointing to where Robin knelt, still playing with the dog.

Unsure what to tell Raven about her father, Holly paused for a moment. Looking into the small girls' big, trusting eyes, she decided that she owed her the truth.

"This is my father, Robin." She said quietly. Robin looked up and smiled at the girl. Raven gasped.

"I know you!" she cried. She looked around frantically at the pictures on the wall. She stared for a moment at the picture of Robin and the small girl, then looked back at Robin. "You're Robin Hood!"

"You see the ring on your finger?" asked Robin, gently.

"It was my grandmother's!"

"I know. It was I who gave it to her. It's a sign of my protection. I have been watching over you and your father as I watched over her. None of your family will ever be alone in this forest."

With Robin's hand clasped in one of Raven's and Holly's in the other, the three walked outside. As they stood in the clearing outside the cottage, Raven began to cry uncontrollably. Robin knelt down and put his arms around her tenderly.

"You're father loved you very much," he told her.

"But I never got to say goodbye," she sobbed.

Silently, Holly reflected on her own experience which had proven to her that this goodbye was not forever, but Raven was so young with so many years in front of her that Holly felt the prospect of a distant reunion at the end of her own life would seem like a poor consolation. Her heart jumped to her throat once more as she realised that, while Raven had maybe fifty or sixty summers at most before she was reunited with her father, she had no idea when, if ever, she would get to see Robert again. She tried to push the thought from her mind, telling her that a love as strong as theirs had to be more powerful than the rules that governed mortal existence. It may take centuries but she knew, had to believe, that one day she and Robert would be together again. Robin placed his hand gently over the centre of Raven's chest.

"Do you know what this is?" he asked kindly, feeling the rapid, distressed beat. Raven looked up at him, her dark eyes wide and full of questioning. Robin continued:

"This is your heart. This is where love resides. When we love someone they become imprinted on our heart and can never be taken away."

Raven looked confused, but she had stopped crying and was now listening to Robin with rapt awe.

"Your father may not be with you in a physical body any more but he will never leave you. Throughout your life you will hear his voice. Sometimes through another's mouth, sometimes in your heart and perhaps you may even hear him in the words you speak to others. He is a part of you now."

The two girls sat on the leafy ground, Holly holding the smaller girl close to her, while Robin went back into the cottage. Moments later he returned carrying the large bundle that had lain by the fire. At this sight, tears began to well up in Raven's eyes again. Holly stroked her hair reassuringly.

"That's not your father he's carrying," she said softly, "It's a shell that he's finished with, like an old tunic. It's made from the same substance as the forest all around us. He borrowed it for a while and, now he has no more use for it, he's given it back."

In front of the girls, the forest floor itself began to stir. The multicoloured leaves parted slowly, as if pushed to either side by invisible hands. Gnarled roots began to poke through the soil, writhing and twisting like burned snakes. They spread apart as the leaves had done, dragging the earth away with them, until a deep hole, almost as long as the cottage itself, could be seen in the ground. Some of the leaves fluttered to the bottom, forming a soft bed.

It was onto this bed of leaves that Robin gently lowered the body. Holly held Raven's hand as she watched silently but with an air of contentment, as if she had been soothed by unseen forces, perhaps a hug from her father but one which came from within rather than without.

As Robin stood up, the roots began to coil themselves around the lifeless form, creating what appeared to be a giant cocoon around it until it was no longer visible. Slowly, the soil trickled in from the sides until the ground was smooth once more. The leaves swirled as if lifted by a gust of wind, although the air was still, and settled back down over the exposed earth as if they had never been disturbed.

Neither Holly, Robin nor Raven said anything for some time until the silence was broken by the hound, running out of the cottage, barking happily and jumping up to lick Raven's face, inadvertently knocking her to the ground as he did so.

It was such a spontaneous, happy moment that it completely broke the tension and sadness in the atmosphere and all three laughed as heartily as they had ever done, rolling around happily on the floor with the playful pet.

Autumn became winter and winter became spring, which, in its turn, gave way to summer. The cycle of life continued. Old trees died and new ones grew. The cottage in the forest became forgotten as the clearing gradually filled with new life.

After comforting her a little more and helping her pack her few belongings, Robin had taken Raven to the edge of the forest where they had met one of his mortal allies who had taken Raven and her faithful, if useless, dog to live with her brother in another village. Holly had not seen her since then.

For an immortal, time has little meaning. A century can pass in a second or a day can feel like an eternity. So it was that one day Holly happened upon the cottage and saw that something was different. The clearing was still gone but a path had been cut to the front door. She even saw smoke rising from the chimney in the roof and it seemed like the old, battered wood and clay walls had been repaired.

Fascinated, Holly wondered why someone would have come to live in this strange old cottage in the middle of the forest. Perhaps a peasant who had lost their home or a fugitive who had fled for their life. She saw that the old leather curtain covering the doorway had been replaced by a wooden door which looked as if it was newly made. Holly walked up boldly and tapped upon it.

The door was opened by a tall woman with long black hair. She gasped when she saw Holly standing outside.

"Holly!" she exclaimed, "It's so good to see you! Come in!"

Confused, Holly stepped across the threshold into the familiar cottage. She looked around. The table and stools were still there, now painted a beautiful array of colours like the autumn leaves in the trees. There were woven rugs on the floor replacing the furs and mats that had been there before and in front of the fire slept a large, strong but gentle-looking hunting hound.

Taking in her surroundings, Holly saw that the tapestries of her father's life still adorned the walls but there were new ones, pictures which showed her and her exploits.

The woman sat on a stool and invited Holly to take one. She smiled, almost shyly, at Holly.

"You don't recognise me do you?"

There was something about the woman's smile that was ever so familiar. Holly looked very closely at her. She wondered if it was possible, if that many years could have passed.

"Raven?"

Smiling happily, the woman nodded. She held out her arms and Holly ran across to her and gave her a huge warm hug. She knew this was her friend of so many years ago, but whereas before she had felt like a little sister, now she was more like a mother. The mother that Holly had never had.

"I've never forgotten you." said Raven, pointing to the pictures on the wall, "Whenever travelling storytellers came to the village I would ask them to tell me about you. I'm sure they made up a lot of the stories but they helped me feel close to you."

"But what about you?" asked Holly, "What's happened in your life?"

"I've grown old Holly," Raven replied, "ever so much more than twenty." She pointed over towards one of the beds where Holly saw, for the first time, a small figure asleep.

"That's my little boy," Raven told her. "He's ten years old. My husband is a forester for the King like my father was when I was a child, and now we have a child of her own."

Walking over to the bed, Holly looked at the sleeping boy. Certainly he looked a little like Raven, and surely a little like his father but Holly smiled when she realised who he reminded her of most. She saw in this young boy the man who she had met ever so long ago in that cottage, Raven's father.

"What Robin said was true," said Raven quietly, coming to stand behind Holly. "The people we love are never really gone. I had a wonderful father and it's because of him that I feel I can be a good mother to my son. I hear his voice all the time. In things people say to me, in my heart and yes, even in the things that I say to others."

Before Holly could reply, she was distracted by the door being swung open. A man walked in, his youthful face glowing with the exuberance which comes from the knowledge of a day's work well done, beneath an unruly mop of whitish-grey hair.

"This is my husband," said Raven, putting her arms around him and giving him a kiss, "The greatest forester and craftsman in the greenwood!"

She beckoned Holly over, placing an arm around her shoulders while keeping her other around her man's waist.

"Charlie," she addressed him, "meet Holly, a really old friend of mine!"

"A pleasure!" Charlie replied, a cheeky glint in his eye. Holly was sure that he had heard all the stories and knew exactly who she was.

"Now," said Raven, in a businesslike manner. "I don't know about anyone else but I'm starving. Charlie, grab some bowls. You will stay won't you Holly?"

Delighted, Holly grinned. This was almost like the old days once more.

They sat and enjoyed the delicious meal together while the old friends told each other all that had happened in their lives since their last encounter so very many years ago.

Eventually, Holly decided that the time had come to leave the others to their own company. She hugged both of them and promised that it would not be so long before they saw each other again.

Looking thoughtful for a moment, Raven reached up and took one of the pictures from the wall. Holly did not see the image but Raven rolled it up and gave it to her.

"Here," she said, "I want you to take this."

Taking the fabric scroll, Holly went to open it but Raven held out a hand to stop her.

"Not now," said Raven, "look at it when you're on your own and whenever you feel lonely."

Deeply intrigued, Holly could not imagine what was in the picture but she tucked it under her arm, gave Raven another hug and returned to the forest.

As the sun set above the trees, Holly sat on a rock by the pond and unrolled the picture. She saw herself in the forest, with her father on one side holding her hand and on the other side was her beloved Robert. Holly clutched the picture to her heart for a moment then looked again. Peeping out from behind a tree in the background was a small girl with long tangled black hair.

The End

Years passed and the years became centuries. For immortal beings, time has little meaning.

There were dark times and there were times of goodness, for as Robert had said, evil can never prevail while one soul knows how to love, for with love comes hope.

But times move on. The world changed. Love became something prized by very few, for what monetary or material value does it have? How many would choose hope over profit?

Robert was not the last good man, but as the centuries rolled by, there were fewer and fewer like him.

It is said that all it takes for evil to flourish is for good folk to do nothing, and flourish it did.

Holly looked at her father. He sat beneath the great oak tree, the only one left in the whole world. The greenwood in which she had been born was long gone. The last tree was left sticking up out of the hard ground of man-made stone , a simple decoration to most, an almost forgotten monument to what had once been. To Robert and Holly, however, it was far more. It was the final part of the world that they had known, clinging desperately to existence in a world which had lost the battle against evil.

She walked quietly over to him and sat down by his side. The ground was hard and cold beneath her, not like the warm, soft forest floor she had known, the cushion of leaves and soil more comfortable than any mattress. It was gone. The greenwood was gone. The water was gone. Soon the last tree would go too, its life sapped by their loneliness. Soon it would all be gone.

All their friends were gone. John had died many, many years ago. He had become weaker with every tree that was destroyed. The once mighty giant had been reduced to a sickly child that even Robin's gift of life-energy could not save. He had died in his friend's arms and his body had fallen apart like rotted old dead wood. Ket and Hob were gone, their world destroyed and them with it.

The singers and storytellers of the age no longer told the stories of bold Robin Hood. He, like the forest he inhabited, was a distant memory, forgotten footnotes in faded books of folklore. He was forgotten. To all intents and purposes he might as well be dead too, yet there he sat. Not alive yet unable to die.

For the first time, Holly thought that her father, an ageless immortal, looked ever so old. It was as if all hope and fight had been drained from him. She placed her hand on his shoulder.

"Do you still believe, father?" she asked. "Do you believe there is still hope?"

Finding himself unable to meet his daughter's eye, Robin gazed into the distance, remembering when the forest, his home, had stretched as far as he could see in every direction. Now he could not even see one other tree. They were gone. His home was gone. His world was gone.

"No. Not any more." He confessed. "I used to believe. I believed that as long as there was beauty and goodness in the world, there was hope for the future."

"But why has that changed?" Holly asked. "Why should that not still be so?"

Swinging his head round, Robin glared at her, his green eyes glowing with that terrible fire, the fire with which he had burned and destroyed so much evil. The fire that burned in his eyes when he felt great anger, hatred or pain. His voice was tight, as if the words were forcing themselves painfully out of his throat. He did not raise his voice but the intensity of his tone made Holly cringe and shrink back.

"Because there is no beauty of goodness left!" He exclaimed. "Look around you! Look at the world! It's gone. All of it. The Dark Spirit has won. The world is full of hatred, ugliness, pain and cruelty. There is no hope for the future because there can be no future. The mortal world has destroyed itself. It is dead. All that's left is the rotting corpse, mocking the life it once contained."

"But you are good," Holly pleaded, "for centuries you have been a symbol to those people who believed as you did. A symbol of hope and goodness."

Robin smiled sadly.

"No, dear child." He said. "I am not good. I do good, but inside I am corrupt and as evil as any other man. More so perhaps. All the evil that exists in the world is ultimately caused by my hand. My selfishness and anger. Perhaps the only difference between a good man and an evil one is the choices we make, and anyway, where had it led us to?"

He looked down at his daughter, the fire gone from his eyes, replaced with a warm, deep glow of tenderness.

"No, my darling. You are the only truly good thing in the world. An immortal child born of pure love. You are all that is left of the goodness which once filled the world, and yet you are not of this world."

He looked away again and closed his eyes. When he spoke again, his voice was quiet, almost a sigh, with a terrible sadness, as if he had lost something very precious or something inside him had died.

"I've failed." He said. "I was supposed to protect the world, to stop all this! But what have I done? Just sat by and watched it happen. Watched the life drain from the world until there was nothing left. People speak of Hell as a realm below but it is here. People have made it for themselves and now we are all stuck here forever."

"Not forever." Holly whispered softly, remembering her mother and the tranquil paradise in which they had met ever so long ago. Robin turned to look at her again, his eyes dull and sad.

"This Hell is not forever." Holly repeated, quietly but surely. "I've seen another world. A world beyond this mortal realm. A world where there is nothing but truth, beauty and love."

"I know, my dear child," he stroked her hair and kissed her gently on the forehead, "I wish I could go there, leave this place behind, but I am pledged to stay for all eternity, until the world is good once more. If there were a way..."

"But there is!" insisted Holly, "Don't you understand? That place is not somewhere else, it is here! The mortal world is filled with evil and sadness but beyond the mortal world lies the Eternal Forest."

"What are you saying?" Robin asked, intrigued. "The only way mortals may reach the Eternal Forest is by leaving the mortal world behind, I cannot bring it here."

"No," Holly agreed, patiently waiting for her father to realise what she was suggesting, "You cannot bring the Eternal Forest to the mortal world but..." she broke off as Robin leapt to his feet, his youthful vigour restored.

"I can bring the mortal world into it!" he declared, punching the air triumphantly. "All this time I thought I was losing, that the Dark Spirit was defeating me but all the time it was hastening its own destruction for when something mortal is destroyed..."

"It becomes immortal!" Holly finished her father's sentence, delighted that he seemed finally to understand. "Then bring it to an end, Father," she pleaded, "Pull the life from the last tree. Cut the rope the corpse is hanging from. Allow this world to go. End its pain. End all of our pain."

"Can this really be the answer?" Robin asked, almost to himself, "After all this time can it be so simple?"

With a deep breath, he placed his hands against the gnarled bark of the oak beneath which they had sat, bark scarred by centuries of abuse and neglect.

"Forgive me, old friend." he whispered, leaning towards the tree.

Using the power he had used so often before to regenerate life, the very power he had used to create Holly in Marian's womb, Robin felt the weak and faltering life energy flowing through the wood of the ancient and once proud oak. He felt the flow of life deeper, followed it down through the roots where they intertwined with the roots of the scant remaining trees and plants. He followed the energy deeper, deeper than he had ever gone before. Where he had once felt the mighty throb of an infinitely powerful heart there were now just the final stuttering beats of a dying creature, of a dying world.

Many times in the past, Robin had used this power to revive that which was dead, digging beyond death to the place where the spark of life survived then drawing it up to refresh the life of the animal or plant he touched. This time was different. This time he dug deeper and found the centre of the world, the feeble, dying spark from which all life drew its strength, and snuffed it out.

If anyone had been able to observe what happened in that instant, they would have seen the world around them turn to grey as the final vestiges of colour drained. Buildings, mountains, all things once so solid became as insubstantial as smoke which hung in the air for a moment before spreading out, losing any trace of its former shape and finally disappearing entirely. The mortal world was gone.

Had they been able to see the moment after that, the observer would perceive what appeared to be an echo of the world that had passed, like an imprint on the memory. But then they would realise that this new world was in fact more real than the last, as if the world which had passed away were simply a faded echo of the one to come.

The atmosphere felt different. Robin felt the warmth of the sun and the breeze on his skin, a sensation he had not experienced since his mortal lifetime when the world was young. The air smelled different too, pure and clean. Robin opened his eyes. He stood with his hands still against the tree, but the tree had changed. Not that it was less than it had been, but more. It was as if it was now the tree it could have been in a world free from disease, harsh weather and vandalism. He opened his eyes in alarm and stepped backwards. Holly stood by his side, gazing in wonder at the Eternal Forest which had appeared around them, even more beautiful than she remembered.

A massive hand clapped Robin on the shoulder. He swung around to find himself face to face, or rather face to chest, with Little John. Larger, stronger and healthier than he had ever seen him. John let out a hearty laugh.

"Welcome brother!" he bellowed, his voice resonant, bouncing off the trees, all of which seemed a little more green and a little more vibrant than any Robin had ever known.

They were all there. John, Ket, Hob and the mortals Much, Alan-a-Dale and the old man Tuck, now young and straight-backed, his once-white beard dark and bushy. There too was Robert. The mortal man he had loved both as a brother and as a son. The man who had carried his name from legend into history.

As she saw Robert, Holly's heart gave a leap. She had known that he would be here but deep down in her heart she had hardly dared to believe it. The pain of losing him the first time had been more dreadful than anything she had ever encountered before or since, and having her hopes of the longed-for reunion dashed would have been unbearable.

She flung her arms around his neck and he took her up in his strong arms.

"I've missed you!" he whispered in her ear as she nuzzled his neck, her fingers wrapped in his long dark hair.

"Oh Robert!" she almost sobbed, "Please don't ever let go of me!" Robert kissed her tenderly before replying.

"That may be a little tricky," he grinned, "as I think there's someone else here wanting a hug!"

"Oh?" Holly looked around. "Who...?" she broke off as she saw the couple who stood a few yards away, holding hands and smiling at her. A tall, golden-haired man and a beautiful young woman with long auburn hair. The woman raised her hand and waved at Holly, her face altering for just a second from youthful beauty to warm, kindly old age before returning to normal.

"Granny!" squealed Holly as Robert set her down on her feet. She ran to the woman who had cared for her in her childhood and flung her arms around her. Granny hugged her tight and kissed her. "You look so beautiful!" Holly exclaimed, tracing the lines of the woman's face with her fingers.

"So do you!" Granny kissed her again. "And who's your handsome friend?" Robert had followed at a more sedate pace and now stood behind Holly.

"This is Robert!" Holly nearly pulled his arm out of his socket as she pulled him forward. "Robert this is..." she paused, "It seems odd calling you Granny now you're so young!"

The beautiful woman smiled warmly. "I'm the same person I always was," she assured Holly, "I will always be your Granny but," she stood up and smiled at Robert, "My name is Eloise and this is my husband Geoffrey."

"It's a pleasure to meet you," Robert beamed, embracing both as if they were long-lost family, "And now," he picked Holly up again, "There's some people over here I'd like you to meet."

Smiling, he carried her a short distance away to where a group of people were becoming reacquainted after generations of separation. They were all young, healthy and strong, and the resemblance to Robert was unmistakeable – they were clearly his family.

In the distance, Holly could see a figure standing alone, watching all that was happening. They did not seem to be with any particular group or family but everyone that passed was greeting them as if they had known them well. Perhaps it was the distance but Holly could not make out if the figure was a man or woman. She seemed to see both a young bearded man and a beautiful young woman at the same time as if two people were occupying the same space or that the figure was somehow both. With a jolt of surprise and her heart filled with joy, Holly realised who the figure was. She knew that this was their forest, a garden like they had planted before, so very long ago. She waved happily at the Creator who returned the greeting, a huge smile on their face as they watched the joyful reunions.

Wild with joy and anxious to greet everyone, Robin ran from person to person. They were all there, everyone who had ever lived. Young, strong, healthy and purified, purged of those dark and haunting feelings and emotions that mar so many otherwise happy lives, with the capacity only to love. There was no place for darkness or evil in this place. How could there be in a place of such pure goodness and love?

They all greeted one another, embracing joyfully. Old friendships were revived and new ones were forged. Rivalries and past hurts forgotten. Families separated by death or geography were all together in the same place, countless generations all together for the first time and forever, never to be separated again.

Even Robin's brother, the face that had haunted him since before time was recorded, was there. Robin expected a rebuke, but he saw only love in his brother's eyes. They hugged warmly – brothers again for the first time in countless centuries.

"Our mother and father?" Robin asked. "Are they...?"

"They're here!" his brother assured him, embracing him once more. "They are ever so proud of you and cannot wait to tell you. But first," he grinned, "There's someone who will positively burst if they have to wait any longer."

Spinning around, Robin scanned the crowds for that one special person. The one person he longed to see more than any other.

"Hello Robin." Marian's voice came soft and gentle as the breeze, caressing his ears with its sweet music.

Feeling like his heart would explode, Robin ran towards her and she to him. He wrapped his arms around her and felt the warmth of her body against his as he had never been able to when they were together before, when she had been a mortal girl and he an immortal spirit. Yet here they were the same, immortal yet physical. Not immortal spirits in the mortal world but immortal beings in a world which was also immortal, seemingly without beginning or end, for already the memory of the world before was fading. Those who remembered it at all thought of it only as a bad dream from which they had awoken to blissful reality.

Pulling Robert by the hand, Holly ran to join her parents and they stood there together, beneath the mighty oak in the Eternal Forest. A family, together at last and for all eternity.

Thanks

To Rick Fenn and Peter Howarth for making Robin Hood
an integral part of my life, through childhood and beyond, with their
wonderful musical:
"Robin, Prince of Sherwood"

To Joel, for keeping this project alive
when things looked bleak

To Raven, for always believing

And
to my sweet forest rose,
for teaching me to believe again

9397402R00071

Printed in Great Britain
by Amazon.co.uk, Ltd.,
Marston Gate.